The Bully's Dare

ADORA CROOKS

* * *

Sign up to get newsletter alerts (plus you get a free MMF romance).

Join the club  https://adoracrooksbooks.com/gift

PART I

THE DARE: SUMMER, 2005

1

———————

KENZI

He's the most beautiful boy I've ever seen.

Raven-black hair cut short around his ears. Sky-blue eyes underneath dark, pensive eyebrows. Lips that are just a little too big for his face. Dimples when he smiles.

He sticks out from the pack—but how could he not?—well over six feet tall and towering over everyone. His body is all lean muscle, and he shows it off under the summer sun, wearing nothing but black boardshorts. He's sitting on the deck of a fishing boat, perched on the rim, like it's a throne, surrounded by a cawing group of three boys and two girls, all in swimsuit attire and drinking wine coolers and shitty beer. They're blasting some Top 40, and it's echoing up and down the sleepy dock of Hannsett Island Marina.

At eighteen, he's been dropped into the body of a god, and it's clear from his posse and his confident grin that he's decided to wield his newfound power by the way of Dionysus—chaos, destruction, and *boys will be boys*.

And I'm bored enough to be entranced by his peacocking.

The only thing I'm working on is a tan, playing through my new Gwen Stefani album, and a rereading of *Little Women* (don't we all want to be Jo?).

3

I'm lying on a towel, Walkman by my side, sprawled out on the top of Four's sailboat, *Sweet Serenity*, which is currently tied up in a slip directly across from the party boat.

Four and Pearl are downstairs (or "below deck" as Four likes to correct me), and every now and then I can hear the blender roar as they down margaritas.

"Four" is short for "stepdad number four."

Which is all he will be, until stepdad number five.

It's not that I have anything against him—he taught me blackjack and he smokes Cuban cigars and he wears his hair in a long gray ponytail which he somehow pulls off. It's just that he's temporary, and there's no point in getting attached to something that won't be around for very long, anyway.

He owns both a beach house and a sailboat at Hannsett Island, an island off Long Island that you have to take a ferry in order to get to, which means that Pearl and I are basically stranded here for the summer. Pearl is my mom, but I haven't called her "mom" since I was five. I have a very vivid memory of her breaking me of the habit in Gabriel's Butchery on the Upper West Side, after I'd ruined her effort to pick up a man in a black tweed turtleneck along with her black-pepper ground salami. Apparently, it's hard to flirt when you have a little rug rat tugging on your dress begging for attention.

Getting out of the stink and hot asphalt of a New York City summer seemed like a great idea at the time. Until I realized that Pearl and Four were going to be the ones drinking and necking...while I got stuck with no friends, limited internet access, and skin that burns before it tans.

It would be better if I wasn't here. I get that. This is Pearl and Four's romantic getaway. I'm the annoying teenager who gets pissy when she's gone more than twenty-four hours without her Myspace account.

My captivity is made only marginally better by the eye candy in slip 12A. I glance over the top of my book. Raven-Hair has got his legs splayed out, leaning back on his elbows, a posture that says *I own this room and everyone in it*. His friends address him as "King," and I can't tell yet if that's his name or if that's just his Holier Than Thou title.

God save us from the cockiness of a teenage boy.

I don't usually go gaga for jocks—they're too often assholes to girls like me, who got curvier once puberty hit. But there's something about his swagger that goes right between my legs. Maybe they grow boys differently in Long Island. Something in the water?

Or maybe it's just me. Nearly eighteen, never been kissed, hormones rocketing through me, making me boy-crazy, making me more of an *Amy* than a *Jo*.

King's boat is a tall motorboat with the words *Healing Touch* scrawled in gold cursive along the back. The engine is going now, gurgling, and it looks like they're getting ready to set off, even though I don't see any adults on board. Are they even old enough to drive that thing? And aren't they all at least semi-buzzed?

The water, I've learned, is lawless.

Curious, I move a headphone off my ear so I can snoop.

The dock boy unhooks the boat from the dock, untangling the lines and tossing them into the boat. Two more boys (obviously part of the party crew) come down the dock with a cooler between them.

"Get over here!" one of the girls shouts from the boat. "Or we'll leave you!"

I watch as the boys comically scramble over the side of the boat, carting the goods over first before tumbling in. Just as the final jock makes his landing, he puts his hand on the dock boy's chest. "Thanks, Dick Boy," I hear him sneer before giving the kid a shove. He goes tumbling backward and hits the water—much to the delight of everyone on board, who breaks into laughter.

Oh, *hell* no. I leap to my feet and throw a single barbed insult: "Assholes!"

It lands straight between the eyes of King, who—*now*—suddenly notices me. His eyes meet mine. They're way, way too blue to be real. His gaze feels like a bolt of lightning striking down my spine. It's hitting 90 degrees right now, yet my nipples are knots.

He gives me a cocky half-grin and shrugs a single shoulder as if to say, *Whoops.*

I feel the heat rise up my neck. Jerk.

The *Healing Touch* glugs as it leaves the slip, and every teenager on board hoots and hollers as they go further out to sea. I hope a kraken swallows them whole, honestly.

I leave my Walkman and book behind and leap from the edge of the sailboat to the wooden dock. The sun-charred slabs are stingingly hot underneath my bare feet, but I ignore the pain and crouch down to the edge to extend my hand.

"Need a hand?" I ask as the dock boy swims to the edge of the dock.

"I've got it," he grumbles, but as he scrabbles at the edge to get his footing, it's clear he *doesn't* have it. He takes my arm, and together we pull him up. His uniform—a white polo shirt with a small lighthouse stitched into the chest pocket and khaki pants—is soaked through. I pick a piece of seaweed from his shoulder, and he grimaces about it.

"Those guys are a bag of dicks," I tell him.

"Yeah," he says. "You don't know the half of it."

"Can I get you anything? A towel?"

"I'll live. The clothes aren't the problem." He's got these soft chestnut irises, and they meet my gaze for the first time. "You want to know the real tragedy?"

"Always."

He reaches into his pocket and pulls out a neatly rolled joint, now soaked and limp.

"RIP," he says.

I hold up a finger. "Hold on."

Why, yes. I have tricks up my sleeve. I reach into my

bikini, where I've stashed away my one vice from Four and Pearl: a rolled joint and a lighter. For the moments I really need to escape.

For the first time, Dock Boy smiles. "Hello, new best friend."

"You can call me Kenzi."

* * *

Dock Boy's real name is Donovan. His real age is nineteen. I haven't discovered his real hair color yet, but I know it's not black because he keeps having to towel off his neck when the dark hair dye drips down around his ears.

Hannsett Island Marina is a self-contained ecosystem, complete with its own restaurant (the Blue Heron, accessible by the public) and a slew of private facilities: a general store, a private pool, a communal shower/restroom/locker room, and a laundry room.

There are only two sets of washers and dryers in the laundry room. Donovan sits on one of the washers, I sit on the fold-out table, and we pass my joint back and forth as his clothes tumble dry.

He's wearing only his boxers, but they look enough like a bathing suit that it's somehow not obscene. Doesn't keep me from admiring his body, though. He's lean, not quite stacked like the jocks, but I like the softness of him. He's kept on this thick leather-woven bracelet and a simple chain necklace with a ring on it.

"Promise ring?" I ask and point to it.

He frowns at that. "My mom's wedding ring."

"Divorced?"

"Deceased."

"I'm sorry."

He shrugs, and that's the end of that conversation.

I get it. I have things that *were* my dad's, sort of. Pearl kept his record player and a few tattered albums. I play them sometimes, but only because I like music, not because I liked him. He died when I was just a kid, and the memories I have aren't great ones, so we never had the kind of connection that inspired me to carry around any of his trinkets.

My head is a little hazy, and I swish my legs under the table. I feel small, but not in a bad way. The comfort of careless innocence. "So why do those guys hate you?"

Donovan thins his lips. He taps ash off onto the quarter slot. "I'm a loser. I'm gay. I don't have a yacht or a summer house. Take your pick."

"That's fucked-up. Have you told anyone about it?"

Donovan's eyes sharpen. "*Who*? No one cares. Jason King and his crew of idiots basically run this island."

King. That clicks. "Jason King…is that the tall one?"

"Tall, blue-eyed, and beautiful? That's the one. He's a rare breed of island native. Have you visited the Lighthouse Medical Center yet?"

"Nope, and from the sound of it, I don't want to."

"Good call. It's Hannsett Island's pride and joy, though. And the island's cash cow. Jason's dad owns it, which basically makes him richer than God. They have a mansion in the Dunes. Two boats. And a second house Upstate."

"All hail the Kings," I say which draws a little wry smile from Donovan. He holds out the joint in offering, but I shake my head. I'm already floating. An ant crawls over my knuckles, its tiny legs tickling, and I let it. I watch its perilous odyssey across the back of my hand and then back onto the table.

"Why are the pretty ones always jerks?" I wonder out loud.

I can feel Donovan looking at me. "You don't seem jerkish."

I stick my tongue out at him. He laughs.

2

DONOVAN

Kenzi quickly becomes my favorite part of my day.

Which isn't hard, when my days mostly involve casting off, casting on, buffing the deck, polishing sideboards, rinse, repeat.

I grind polish over fifty-foot yachts until I'm caked in sweat and my fists refuse to unclench. I can usually find Kenzi at the pool or sunbathing on her stepdad's boat, *Sweet Serenity*. She's easy to steal away for a smoke break, or a dip in the pool, or just a chat over watermelon slices and H2O.

Kenzi loves music, above all, and some days we just take turns listening to her Walkman. Eventually, she opens up her notebook and shows me some of the lyrics she's working on. She wants to be a songwriter. Not a singer/songwriter—just a songwriter. Her lyrics are good. Really good. I call her the female Bernie Taupin. She smiles when I say that.

Plus, King's crew tends me leave me alone when I'm with her. So. That's a silver lining.

We talk about our plans for next year—or lack thereof. She's on the waitlist for Berklee College and hasn't heard back, so as far as she's concerned, she's taking a gap year. I can relate—I've been in limbo for the past year as Dad and I try our luck with scholarship lotto. So far, no hits.

Except for Tomorrow's Doctors.

Every summer, the Lighthouse Medical Center runs a four-week program for what they call "Tomorrow's Doctors." Ages 17-19. Throw the minnows in the pond. See if they can swim.

So, after work, I clock out, hop on my bike, and pedal as fast as I can out of the marina, up the road that winds alongside the dunes, all the way to the medical center.

The first thing you see when you approach the medical center is the lighthouse itself. The lighthouse hasn't been in operation for over fifty years, but it's still a beautiful thing. Red brick, restored to its former glory, with a black chrome dome. The light doesn't shine anymore, except for special occasions—holiday light shows, that sort of thing.

The lighthouse is flanked by three buildings: the pediatric wing, the general care and rehabilitation wing, and the emergency wing. I'm hit with the smell of freshly cut grass as I cut across the large lawn to park my bike on the rack. I don't lock my bike here; there's no need. Everyone on the island stays on the island.

I've got my knapsack stuffed in a milk carton my dad looped to the back of my bike for storage, and I quickly throw it on my shoulders before heading inside.

Entering the Lighthouse Medical Center doesn't knock the breath out of me like it used to. But the first couple of times, yeah, it was hard not to be impressed. The lobby sits underneath a domed ceiling, all glass. Through it, you can see the top of the lighthouse.

As soon as the doors open, you come face-to-face with a giant art deco–style sculpture of a man on one knee. He has his hand open, the sun sitting in the palm of his hand. Underneath the sculpture, the words run in a band: "A Guiding Light Through the Dark."

The only thing more impressive than the talented, skilled doctors at Lighthouse Medical Center are the deep pockets of the donors.

It's the kind of money a guy like me can't even begin to wrap my head around.

I grip the straps of my backpack a little tighter and trudge ahead.

Tomorrow's Doctors meet on the second level of the rehab wing, which is otherwise blocked off for professionals. It's mostly storage here—a lot of doors marked "Keep Out." Labs with expensive equipment. I walk down the hall, to the doctors' mess. There's a kitchenette here, complete with a coffee machine, a small fridge, and a snack machine. In the adjoining room are bunk beds for the on-call doctors who pull long hours. The lockers that line the room are meant for the staff, but Tomorrow's Doctors get six spots reserved at the far end.

I'm not the only one here. The cast are as follows:

Jason: the leader of the pack, his father's prodigy.

Nick: Jason's best friend, stocky, the kind of guy who will argue with you that his shirt is *salmon*, not pink.

Brett: a blond-haired jock, usually found strutting around with a volleyball.

They're loitering around the circular table. Nick has taken a bag of Doritos from the snack pile, and it makes his fingers orange.

"C'mon, Jason," Nick is whining. "Throw us a bone."

"A gentleman never tells," I hear Jason say.

"Since when are you a gentleman?" Brett protests. "Spill."

I go to my own locker, pop it open, and start to shove my things in it.

"I *can* tell you one thing," Jason gives in.

"What?"

"Her sister was better."

Gross. His friends howl with laughter, but I have a hard

time hiding my disdain. My locker rattles when I slam it, and I hear their laughter come to a halt.

"Hey, Nick," Jason says, "does something smell fishy to you?"

"Yeah," Nick says, "smells like the whole fresh market just walked in."

My jaw clenches. I keep my eyes on the floor, keep my back to them, and ignore their obnoxious cackles as I enter the adjoining room.

We take our class sessions in a repurposed conference room, with a long oval table surrounded by black swivel chairs. The other two students have already taken their seats, notebooks open. I wouldn't call them friends. No one is exactly *friendly* to me, since King and his clan put a target on my back last summer and therefore fraternizing with me is social suicide.

It wasn't always like this. Believe or not, Jason and I used to be almost-friends. Between the beachgoers and the patients in and out of the clinic, Hannsett is an island of transplants. No one stays here very long.

Except for me and Jason. We're a rarity. Year-around natives. Hannsett Island is like a prison—you love the one you're with. Before he surrounded himself with summer partygoers who call him *King* and decided he preferred obnoxious boat parties, frat boys, and picking on anyone he considered an easy target.

Which included me.

I sit next to Ernest, who is quiet and generally ignores me, which I'll take over taunting. Even he rolls his chair a little further away from me today, though.

I did spend half of the day cleaning a fishing boat. Maybe I do smell like chum.

Eventually, Jason's crew takes their seats, and our teacher arrives. Dr. Esmeralda is a middle-aged Black woman who has been at the hospital as long as I have. She was here when my mom got sick, so I feel like I already know her. She has a warm bedside manner, but she's stoic in the classroom.

"Let's see who did the precursory reading," she says once we're all settled in. "Three patients enter the emergency room with heat-related illnesses—something we get a lot of at Hannsett. The first patient is seventy-two, has fainted, and feels dizzy. The second patient is a homeless man, who seems confused and exhibits poor coordination; he also has hot, dry skin. The third is a swimmer with tachycardia and nausea. Who do you see first?"

Her eyes scan the room. Then they land on— "Jason."

Jason lifts his head from his notebook. He blinks as though he's come out of a dream. "Um…"

"*Um?* That isn't a diagnosis I've ever heard of."

A ripple of laughter across the room. Jason isn't laughing, though. He has the look of a bull post-matador fight. Wounded. Tired. And plotting to run everyone through with his horns as soon as he gets his strength back.

"Can you repeat the question?" he asks.

"No." Dr. Esmerelda's gaze swings over to me. "Donovan."

"I'd treat the homeless patient first," I recite immediately. "The temperature of his skin suggests heat stroke, which can be life threatening for someone in his condition."

"Seems you have a guardian angel, Jason," Dr. Esmerelda says. "Donovan just resurrected your patient. Let's spend less time hitting the beach this summer and more time hitting the books."

I can feel Jason's stare, like ice chips sliding down my spine.

I ignore it and press my pen deep into the paper, making a welt in my journal. I'm going to pay for opening my big dumb mouth later, but..

At least my hypothetical patient lived.

* * *

I make a beeline to my locker after class. Jason and his crew are loitering. Jason is sitting on the counter with his shoes on the table.

Respect is for lesser humans, apparently.

He looks at me, and there's a glint in his eyes I don't like.

"Sup, Angel?" he asks.

Angel. Jesus Christ. I guess I have Dr. Esmerelda to thank for my new nickname now.

I ignore him and go to my locker.

"Hey," Brett chimes in, "King is talking to you."

My jaw clenches. *Let's rip this Band-Aid.* "What?"

"What're you doing tonight? You wanna come out?"

"Out?" I repeat skeptically.

"Yeah. We're having a party tonight."

Is Jason…inviting me to a party? Seems unlikely. His impossibly tall frame is arched over, one leg crooked on a chair. He's panther-like and coy in his body language, his knees slightly splayed, his broad shoulders angled back. His tight pants do nothing to hide the package underneath, and I hate myself for noticing these details about him.

His body language always makes him look like he's flirting…even when he isn't.

His wolf's grin makes me suspicious.

"Good for you," I say.

"So you coming?"

I consider my options. I should say no. On the other hand. If this is a genuine invitation, a party might be fun. When was the last time I was invited to something like that—?

Never. The answer is never.

"Maybe," I say as I open my locker, "I'll have to check with—"

But as soon as the door swings open, two wet bodies fly out at me. Huge, slippery bass flip out of my locker and slap against my chest. The smell that my locker unleashes is atrocious.

Jason and his crew cackles. I feel Jason's hand slap on my shoulder. "You know what?" he says. "Maybe next time. Think you should go home and…shower this off." He steps backward out the door. Before he leaves, he has the audacity to wink. "Later, Angel."

The dead fish leak onto the ground. So much for sterilization.

Fucking dick.

* * *

Every muscle in my body hurts as I bike back to the marina.

Sunsets are beautiful at Hannsett Island. Pink and lavender streaks across the sky and spills across the water. The boats sway softly, each tucked away safely in their slip. We have a pair of swans that nest in the tallgrass every year and they make small ripples in the glass-like water. Every now and then, a gull calls out or a mainline bangs against the mast, giving out a gong-like sound. Other than that, it's still. Quiet.

Paradise is nice—if you're rich enough to enjoy it. My dad and I live in a trailer. It's tucked away behind the pool. They don't let us park it in the parking lot, "too unsightly" for the boat owners. Instead, we're hidden behind the pine trees, in a strip of dirt where grass once was.

I roll my bike through the thicket and rest it against a tree. Dad is cooking up dinner on the BBQ, and the smell of burning meat makes my stomach pinch.

"Dinner's ready in five," Dad says.

Things dad never says:

How was your day?

Are those boys still taunting you?

Why do you smell like fish?

Why do you smell like pot?

Is everything okay?

Our conversations are mostly functional: can you do this? / this is done. Food is ready / pass the ketchup.

Which is fine. He's got skin like leather from being in the sun and looks twice as old as he should. He's as exhausted as I am. We don't have the time or energy for a heart-to-heart.

"Be right there," I say. I start inside the trailer. We have a jar we share, and I dump my tips in it. It's not much, but we'll stay fed for the rest of the week.

Our trailer has a sink in the front, a cushioned bench (my bed), a bathroom, and a main cabin in the back (Dad's bed). I stretch across the bench and lie down. Just for a second, I tell myself.

But as soon as my eyes close, I'm out.

I don't know how long I've slept, but I wake up to my father's hand on my shoulder. Rough hands, gentle squeeze. "Hey, kiddo," he murmurs. "Some girl is here to see you."

I blink awake, disoriented. My hair is a mess. I'm still in my sweat-stained uniform. I'm not fit for humans. A girl?

Only one girl it could be. I descend the steps and glance around.

Kenzi stands there. She's wearing a cute yellow dress with strappy shoulders. Her black hair is in swoopy waves. Green eyes shining like sea glass.

The sight of her makes me feel a weird way, a way I don't usually feel about girls. My heart launches itself against my chest like a wild animal suddenly uncaged.

"What's up?" I ask. Casual.

She half-grins, looking shy—my father usually has that effect on people; he's hard-edged and scary. But she holds up a paper plate, a piece of cake on it, and says, "I come bearing gifts."

She's a gift: pristine and pretty, fresh off the spotless deck of her stepdad's boat.

I'm filthy and burningly aware of the eyesore that is the trailer.

I sway on the balls of my feet, deliberating. "Give me one second."

I close the door on her and squeeze past my dad. "You want me to tell her to go?" he asks.

"No." I'm tearing off my clothes, ripping a paper towel off, dampening it, and wetting my face, the back of my neck, all the parts of me that feel grimy. I pull on black jeans, a black shirt. Run my fingers through my hair. I slip my lip ring into my bottom lip—I have to take it out while I work (Mr. King's orders), but I try to pop it in once I'm off to keep the hole from closing up.

"Your burger is still on the grill," Dad reminds me.

"Thanks. I'll grab it later."

I slip outside and close the door behind me. No more dock boy.

Kenzi is sitting on my stump. She glances up, and her eyes sweep over me. "So this is what Donovans look like in their natural habitat."

"Mmhm." There's a sugar flower on her slice of cake, and I swipe it between my fingers and pop it in my mouth. "Whose birthday is it?"

"Mine."

I squint at her. "Are you serious?"

"Lucky number eighteen."

"That's a big one."

"So I've been told." If she's put off by the trailer, BBQ pit, or my growly father, she doesn't show it. The opposite, actually; she looks right at home.

"Wanna take a walk?" I ask her.

"Sure."

She hands over the plate and a plastic fork, and we walk through the grass and behind the fenced-in pool.

The crickets sing. Fireflies blink. We find a large slab of

stone to sit on. We watch an egret wade her long legs through the tall grass at the edge of the water.

All of this nighttime peace is interrupted only by the true wildlife of Hannsett Island: the *Healing Touch* is booming tonight, blaring loud pop music.

Jason King and his merry band of popular kids never quit.

"Wanna play a game?" Kenzi asks as we pick at the cake.

"Sure."

"Truth or dare?"

"Dare."

"I dare you to catch a firefly."

"Hold this." I hand her the plate, and she takes it. I get up and move just a little ways into the long cattail bushes. There's a bunch of small lights, blinking on and off. Fireflies are pretty, but dumb and slow. I cup one in both my hands, then come back over to Kenzi.

"Check it out." I open my hands, just a little. She leans over, her head nearly bumping mine. Inside my curved fingers, the trapped firefly glows, illuminating my palms.

"Nice," Kenzi murmurs. Her breath warms my hands.

"You want to glow?" I ask her.

She narrows her eyes at me. "What, like rip his butt off and rub it on our faces?"

"Well—"

"Psychopath. Let it go."

"Your lucky day, little guy," I tell him. I open my hands, and the firefly flies out, waving drunkenly through the sky.

"Your turn," I tell Kenzi as we sit back down on the stone. "Truth or dare?"

"Truth," she says, which I think is brave.

"What's the one thing you want to do now that you're eighteen?"

She lets out a small laugh and rubs the back of her neck. "Honestly?"

"That's why it's called *truth.*"

"Okay. I want to lose my virginity." She shrugs. "I know that's like…pedestrian."

"It's not."

"And I know it's a *big deal* for some people. But I don't know…I just sort of want to rip off the Band-Aid. You know?"

"Quick and fast?"

"Okay, maybe not *that* much like ripping off a Band-Aid. But just…simple. No complications. With someone I trust, ideally. And then it'll be over with, and I can go about my life without this *thing* hanging over my head." Her emerald eyes blink at me. "Do you think I'm cold?"

"No," I tell her. "It's your body. You should do whatever you want with it."

She points her fork at me. "Thank you. You *get* me."

And I get it: I'm her gay best friend who she can open up to about things like this. Her blossoming sexuality. Her slutty summer plans. I am a man she can talk to fearlessly, without worrying that I'll turn around and try to kiss her.

So why is this conversation making me hard?

'Okay, you now," she says.

"What about me?"

"Truth or dare, Donovan?"

As if truth is even an option right now. "Dare."

She nods toward the party boat. "I dare you to give them a taste of their own medicine."

An idea forms. I put down the paper plate and stand up. "Only if you come with me."

"Obviously, I'm in." I reach out a hand, and she takes it. Her hand feels so soft in mine.

* * *

I lead Kenzi down the dock.

It's illuminated by dock lights, these big, bulky things that are swamped by moths. We walk slowly down the wooden panels so they don't creak too loudly.

It turns out to be overkill. By time we get to the *Healing Touch*, we don't see anyone on the back—they've moved the party to the bow of the boat. We can hear beer cans cracking, music blaring, and rancorous laughter, but we can't see them…

And more importantly, they can't see us.

I point to the cleats, which keep the boat tied up to the dock. "You get the ones on the other side," I whisper to Kenzi. "I'll take these."

She sneaks around the side of the boat. I crouch down on the edge of the dock and unwind the thick rope from the cleats. As quietly as I can, I toss the rope onto the deck of the boat.

Kenzi comes back around, crouching behind the lights. "Done!"

I put my palms on the side of the boat. "On the count of three…push."

I count, and together, we give the boat a hefty push. It doesn't take much. It's a still night, and soundlessly, slowly, the boat follows the momentum of our push and drifts out of the slip and into the inky black water.

In the enclosed marina…it's not going far. But it's going to give them a hell of a shock when they realize what's going on.

Which happens sooner than I think.

"Whoa, are we moving, or is it just me?" a female voice hiccups from the bow.

"Run!" I whisper urgently to Kenzi.

We race down the dock, up the bridge, and behind the tall cattails by the pool. The tall grass tickles our ankles. We collide together, and I hook my arm around her to slow her down. "Look," I tell her.

Between the cattail reeds, we can see the chaos below.

The *Healing Touch* floats around aimlessly and lists toward one of the yachts. There are shouts from the jocks, then shouts from the people on the yacht, and they take out long poles in attempt to push the *Healing Touch* away before the two boats bump. The *Healing Touch* starts drifting away from the yacht then…and straight into a mudbank.

I can feel Kenzi's warm breath on my neck. Her heart is beating so fast I can feel it, tiny thumps against my bare arm. "Oh my God…" she says. "I'm sorry if you get in trouble for that."

"You kidding?" I tell her. "This is the best night of my life."

I could kiss her right now.

It's an urge, tugging on me, my heart strung like a marionette.

I could kiss her. We're so close like this. Her eyes meet mine, and for a second, I think she's thinking the same thing.

And then a splash catches our attention. We look back to the boat. Jason and Nick are in the mud now, water up to their waists, trying to push the boat back out. The boat makes a terrible grinding noise as someone tries to start up the engine. Jason King's swears can be heard all throughout the marina.

Kenzi puts her hand on her mouth and laughs.

The moment is gone, but we don't break apart.

We stay like this, locked together, watching the well-earned comedy play out below.

3

———

JASON

*Y*ou've caught me.

I'm an asshole. A Grade A bully. A jerk in sheep's clothing.

Meanness is a pin stuck between my shoulder blades, and I can't reach to get it out.

I swim until I can't feel the pin anymore. Until I can't feel anything but searing heat in my arms. Cramps in my legs. Lungs that feel like they're going to burst.

Finally, I pull myself back onto shore. Salt and sand cling to me.

It's a beautiful goddamn day on Hannsett Island. Like every summer day.

Bayside Beach is packed. Families under huge, multicolored umbrellas. People playing Frisbee. Volleyball. Seagulls fighting over french fries.

Amy lies sprawled across a beach towel, *Cosmo* magazine in her lap. She's wearing a bikini that barely covers her and a hat so big, it's essentially a second umbrella. When I step over her to grab a towel from the bag, she screams, "You're dripping on me!"

"Bet that's not the first time," Nick snickers. Nick sits in the fold-out beach chair, a dollop of sunscreen smeared down his nose, and Amy throws her magazine at him.

I pop open the cooler, but there's nothing but beers in here. "We have any water?"

Nick looks at Amy, who shrugs. I rummage around until I find a hard seltzer. Close enough. I chug that instead as I towel off water from the back of my neck.

"Hey," Nick says, "tell King what you told me."

Amy holds on to her hat and points across the beach. "That's the girl."

My eyes follow her finger. I recognize the girl in question immediately as the newbie from across the dock. She's sitting with her mother and one of my dad's friends—Terry. She's wearing a red one-piece and has headphones on. Big sunglasses on. She's sprawled across the towel, arm draped over her eyes. Blocking out the world.

The sight of her on full display like that—vulnerable, open—it does something to me. I feel my heartbeat pick up, only it's got nothing to do with my swim.

"What about her?" I ask.

Amy looks up at me, lips curled, pleased with herself. "She's the one I saw with Dick Boy. They're like *besties* now or whatever. They took the ropes off your dad's boat and pushed it away."

So *she's* the source of all my trouble. Anger is a heat, not an emotion. It burns and doesn't let up. My pin digs a little deeper.

I clasp my hand over Nick's shoulder to get his attention.

"Get everyone together," I tell him. "Let's do a bonfire tonight."

"Hell yeah!"

"Hey." Amy pops up, her body brushing mine. She has sand stuck all up the back of her arms, and she tickles the tips of her fingers over my bare abdomen. "Wanna come get some ice cream with me?"

The look in her eyes tells me *ice cream* isn't the only thing she wants in her mouth.

But I'm wound too tight. Burning too hot.

"Later," I tell her. "I'm going back in."

I need to clear my head in a way that only salt water can cure. Extinguish this rage before it consumes me. I toss the beach towel back down and dive back into the water.

4

KENZI

*L*ive piano music plays. Candlelight flickers over white tablecloth.

Pearl has dressed me in white. Which is not a good look for me. I look like a cream puff, the dress bunching awkwardly over my tummy. I crush my crème brûlée with my fork.

The Blue Heron is the high-end restaurant that overlooks the marina. It has two entrances, one for the "common folk" of Long Island, and a second entrance exclusively for the boat owners. The restaurant overlooks the marina, and you can see boats swaying in their slips through the siding. The Blue Heron calls itself the best place to catch the sunset on all of Hannsett Island, and they're not wrong.

It's incredibly romantic. And incredibly *awkward* when you're sitting across from your mother and her new catch, who are both caught under the spell of the ambiance.

What is it about candlelight that makes people so disgustingly gooey?

"God, that sunset is beautiful," Pearl muses, touching her manicured nails to her lips.

Four peels her blonde hair from her shoulder and places a

kiss on the bare skin there. "The *second* most beautiful thing here," he muses.

She laughs, a high bell-like sound which is definitely not genuine. I make a vomiting noise.

"*Kenzi.*" Pearl says my name as a warning, her eyes slits.

I pout. I crack another layer of toasted caramel.

Out of the corner of my eye, I see him. Jason King. The temperature practically changes when the King family enters the restaurant.

They're royalty. Jason's father is a salt-and-pepper high-baller—perfectly groomed, wearing a blazer and a watch they could probably see from space. Mrs. King is ageless, tanned, and a Hollywood classic beauty. She's fiddling with the shirt collar of what must be Jason's older brother—they have the same strong jaw, same bright eyes, and the same prowling presence of a cougar.

Jason looks different without his beach boardshorts and his posse. His shirt is buttoned up all the way to his Adam's apple, and the collar looks tight. He's holding his wrist, hands falling about to his groin—classic defensive posture. He's the tallest one in his family, a full head taller than his father, but next to the other man, he's shrunken, somehow. His shoulders are hunched, head half-bowed like a chastised dog.

Jason might be the king of high schoolers, but in his father's shadow, he's a meager *prince*. And it shows.

Mr. King smiles past the concierge, and the owner of the Blue Heron greets him personally with a stiff handshake. I find my eyes following them—the King family has become my new favorite nature documentary. *And here, we see the Kings in the wild, prowling over their domain...*

Blue sapphire eyes meet mine. *Oh shit.* I've been caught staring. I look away just when Jason's penetrating gaze connects with mine. Where to put my eyes? Outside. On the pearly stars. I twist my hair in my fingers.

Out of the corner of my vision, a too-tall figure approaches. "Shit," I whisper under my breath.

"Mr. Blake. Missus P." Jason stands at the edge of our table, polite as a fucking church mouse.

"Jason." Four smiles. He rests his hand on the back of Pearl's neck. "How's it going, son? Is your family here?"

"Yes, sir." Jason's eyes fix on me again. "I'm sorry to interrupt your dinner. Can I have a word with Kenzi?"

I roll my eyes and pick a breadstick off the table. I chew it the way Bugs Bunny might nibble his carrot in front of Elmer—*you're not the boss of me*. "Whatever you have to say, you can say in front of the table," I tell him.

"Okay." His eyes are sparkling. There's that mischief again. He comes out with it: "You're the one who cast off my boat."

He doesn't look pissed. If anything, he looks…amused? There's that smug smirk climbing his lips.

I shrug. "Maybe. Maybe not."

"Wanna come to a bonfire tonight?"

"Oh, a bonfire, honey, that sounds like fun!" Pearl says too enthusiastically.

"*Pearl*," I chastise her. She's completely ruining my cool.

Pearl sighs loudly. "Excuse me for wanting you to have some teenage escapades while you're still young."

Jason eyes me. "I'll drive."

I pretend to consider it. "Can I bring my friend?"

"Who's your friend?"

"Donovan."

A sliver of something cruel slides across Jason's blue eyes. "I don't think he'd like the crowd."

"By that, you mean you don't think the crowd would like him?"

His mouth sets. "Whichever."

I shrug. "Then it doesn't sound like my crowd, either."

I scoop a forkful of crème brûlée while Jason considers. "Okay," he says finally. "He can come."

"Cool. You can pick me up later."

Jason's smile returns. Calm. Controlled. Cocky. "See you then." Then he nods toward Four and Pearl. "Enjoy the rest of your dinner."

With that, he turns and leaves to join his own family again. They have, obviously, the best table in the house, with a perfect view of the boats swaying in the marina.

Pearl puts her lips to her wineglass. "He's cute," she says into her pinot noir and wiggles her eyebrows.

"If you're into...*that*." I shrug and try not to blush.

"What did he mean about his boat?" Four asks, his brow furrowed.

"Hey!" I jump in with a quick change of topic. "I was thinking—can you teach me how to fish tomorrow?"

5

———

DONOVAN

"*K*iddo."

My eyes pry themselves open. As the sleep clears, the Sundance Kid races across the screen, shouting for his partner in crime.

Our TV is a small, square box, which is propped up on the fold-out table in front of us, along with a few empty beers and scraps from dinner.

I've passed out in the crook of my dad's arm. And drooled on myself.

Real baller right here.

Dad points to the window. "Your secret admirer is back."

As if on cue, there's a *plink!* against the window. A muffled voice: "Donovan!"

I jump up and wipe my mouth with the back of my arm. I fling open the door of our trailer.

She's there, looking ethereal in a white dress and a dangerous smile.

I hang halfway out the door. "Hey."

"Hey," she says. Small pile of acorns in her hand. And then: "Wanna come to a party tonight?"

"Sounds gross."

"Which is why I'm inviting you, nimrod."

I stifle a grin. "Okay."

* * *

Jason picks us up in a golf cart. Which is not the ride we expected.

We both changed for the occasion—she's wearing a bathing suit underneath tiny shorts, a Hawaiian shirt, and bright orange sneakers and, somehow, pulls it all off. I'm in my one pair of pants without holes in them, a black button-up with the top buttons undone. Kenzi has also had her fun running a little gel through my hair and adding some liner to my eyes. I don't hate either of it.

Jason is classic prep boy chic, in his polo shirt, khaki pants.

"What, no hot rod?" Kenzi asks as she climbs into the back of the cart. I follow suit, gripping the side.

"It's the only thing my dad lets me drive after I wrecked the Buick." As he starts it back up, Jason adds, "And the Mercedes."

Hannsett Island is a little over five miles long, so it's golf cart–friendly.

Jason drives us to the beach on the east end. The sunset stretches ribbons of orange and pink across the sky and ocean. The air tastes dry and salty.

Hannsett Island has two main beaches: bayside and cliff-side. We're going to the cliffs now, which has choppier surf and therefore is less populated by tourists. The cliffs are made of clay, and after the rain, you can scoop your fingers through it and draw clay tattoos over your skin, like henna.

We can hear the party before we see it. Jason parks, we hop out, and he lifts a huge cooler that clinks when he carries it. Kenzi and I are in charge of the more manageable things— a couple of beach towels, a fold-out chair.

We climb the sand dune. The sun is dying, but we have plenty of light—a roaring bonfire in the middle of the beach. A boombox blares. Someone picks a guitar to an entirely different song. When Jason enters the scene, he's greeted with a war cry. He lifts his hand in acknowledgement. The King settling his buzzed and blazed clan.

This is not my clique—hell, this isn't even the same *species*. They are the rich and beautiful of Hannsett Island. I'm the guy who polishes Daddy's boat.

I feel my feet slow down, toes sinking in the sand the closer we get to the group.

Jason's core gang circles him. He points to me and Kenzi.

"This is Kenzi. Kenzi, this is Nick, Amy, and Brett."

Nick glares at me. "What's Dick Boy doing here?"

I brace for impact.

"I invited him," Jason says, which surprises me. He's claiming me. Then Jason's eyes sweep over Nick. "Go grab him a beer, yeah?"

They're bowing up—two stags with clashing horns. And then Nick breaks.

"Yeah," Nick says. "Okay."

Ah. So this is what it feels like to be blessed by the protection of Saint King himself.

Nick doesn't stop glaring at me, but he obeys, pulling two High Lifes out of the cooler. He hands one to me and one to Kenzi.

I take it and swallow back my small victory. I'm not used to the taste.

Amy—all thin limbs and blonde hair—leans her body into Jason's. She plays with the collar of his shirt. "Can I steal you for a second?"

"Sure," Jason grins. "Be right back."

He won't be *right* back, not if the hungry look in Amy's eyes is any indication as she drags him through the dune grass.

Kenzi plops down next to the guitarist. "So!" she says cheerfully, "Can you play anything other than Kumbaya?"

Kenzi is vivacious and bright. She might not fit the mold —Barbie-doll girls with big tits and empty heads—but she has a cutting wit and is "one of the boys". Maybe they can smell the entitlement on her, like a pheromone. They accept her into the group, and she blends in well.

Meanwhile, I sit beside her, quietly drink my beer, and sift sand between my toes. The lower layer still retains the day's heat.

Eventually, Kenzi and I peel off from the heat of the bonfire. We end up sitting on a dried-out husk of fallen tree, drinking and watching the sea creep up.

Kenzi points at the stars. "That's Big Bird."

"I think you mean Big Bear."

"No. Big Bird. Look at his beak!"

I laugh. The beers have made me hazy. "So I guess you're going to be an astronaut when you get older, huh?"

"I might." She turns to me. "What about you?"

"Doctor."

"Seriously?"

I nod. "It's all I've ever wanted to do. When my mom got sick…chemo and all that. The doctors that took care of her; they were my heroes. I want to do that for someone else."

"That's beautiful."

"Plus. The salary is nice."

"Ah, *there* it is."

We laugh. Out of the corner of my eye, I see Jason leave the bonfire to come join us.

He's lost his shirt, and it's hard to avoid looking at the glint of his muscled abdomen.

"Hey, beautifuls." Jason flops down beside us. He's got his back on the sand, and when he moves, I see it sticking to his shoulder blades.

"I think it's flirting with you, Kenzi," I tell her.

Jason cranes his neck back at us. "You having fun?"

"Not as much fun as you." Kenzi pokes his side with her toes. "You have lipstick on your neck, champ."

Jason rubs the side of his neck. "Is it my color?"

"A little bright."

"Hey," Jason says. "You guys wanna play a game?"

"What?"

"Spin the bottle?" Jason ventures.

"I'd rather give myself a lobotomy," I answer.

"Truth or dare?" Kenzi offers.

Jason snaps his fingers and points at her. "Bingo. Truth or dare, Kenzi?"

She grins. "Dare."

"Alright. I dare you to jump in the water."

Kenzi snorts a laugh. "Alright. Can do."

With that, she stands up and starts unbuttoning her shirt.

Kenzi is a lot of things. *Afraid* isn't one of them.

I grip the neck of my bottle a little tighter as I watch her fingers work off her buttons, one after the other. The firelight is licking at her skin, casting flickering shadows from the downward tilt of her chin, the curves of her breasts.

I remind my body to be still. I remind myself not to lick my lips like a hungry wolf. Everything in me goes rigid, though, when she drops her shirt and wiggles out of her pants.

I try to remind myself that I've seen her in a bathing suit before. But there's something about tonight. The way the bonfire light makes her creamy skin golden. The way her dark hair falls around her shoulders. That small dip in her back, inviting the touch of a hand.

I'm painfully hard. And I'm not alone. Jason watches her undress, his eyes never leaving her.

She glances back at us. Narrows her eyes. A light grin rests on her lips. "What's up? First time seeing a fat girl in a bikini?"

Then she flips us the bird and rushes to the water. There's a whoop from the firepit. She dives into the water, her pearly white body vanishing in the dark water.

For a second, all I can hear is the rushing of my own blood.

"So what's the deal with you two?" Jason asks suddenly.

I weigh the question. "What do you mean?"

"Friends? Dating? Friends with benefits?"

My laugh that escapes me is more like a hiss. My jaw won't unclench.

"Look—it's not any of my business if you're gay. Or bi. Or whatever. But there is something I want you to know." Jason puts his hand on the driftwood. The way we're positioned right now—me, splayed out on the sand, him, hovering over me—it's close, and strangely intimate. Yet he doesn't have any trouble looking me directly in the eyes.

And that is the real power of Jason King. His ability to hang in an uncomfortable situation without even blinking.

"What's that?" I ask.

"I'm going to fuck her." When he says it, he does so bluntly. Matter-of-fact. "Maybe not tonight. But I'm going to fuck her this summer. And I'm going to make her cum. Hard. And when she does, she's going to be screaming my name. Not yours."

Jason pushes back and straightens up. He flashes me a smile. "Enjoy your beer, Angel," he says before heading toward the water.

So much for Mr. Nice Guy. I hug my beer closer and nurse it.

My ears burn. I want to leave, but I'm not leaving without Kenzi, so I sip on my beer and stare off into the water. I catch glimpses of her splashing around. I try to swallow my unease, but the carbonation fizzes in my stomach and brings it back up.

6

JASON

*P*hosphorescence lights up the water as I splash in. It glows like diamonds around my hands and arms as I swim through the ocean.

The water is alive. The beach is alive.

I am alive. Kenzi is alive. We're alive, and young, and beautiful, and I want to put myself inside of her and make love to the swell of the sea.

We tread water. It's cool, but not cold. Nice.

I can hear the muffled sounds of music and laughter from the beach, but we're far enough out that we're swallowed in the dark.

She cocks her head. "Are you following me?"

"Something like that."

"Isn't Amy going to be jealous?"

"Amy isn't my girlfriend."

"Uh-huh." She doesn't look convinced. "So how many not-girlfriends do you have right now?"

I shrug. It's the only honest answer I can give.

"So what am I…the last woman on Hannsett Island that you haven't stuck your dick in?"

"I'm going to say something…and I don't want you to die of shock."

She grins. "I'll brace myself."

"I think you're pretty cool, Kenzi."

"You don't even know me."

"I know some things."

She eyes me suspiciously. "Like what?"

I rattle it off. "You're reading *Little Women*. You hate fishing. You vandalize other people's boats."

She's smiling. I like her smile. "Have you been watching me?"

I dip my chin in the water. "Sounds creepy when you say it like that."

She edges closer to me. Every now and then, I feel her toes brush against my calves, or her knees bump my legs. We're liable to get tangled, treading water like this. Even in the cool water, my blood is rushing hot.

"Do you think I'm pretty?" she asks.

There's something about the question that crushes me right in the heart. I feel my breath leave my lungs. "Yeah. I do."

"Truth or dare, Jason?"

"Dare."

Her forehead touches mine. I can feel the heat of her breath sticking to my wet skin. "I dare you to let me suck you. Right here. Right now."

My voice gets stuck in my throat. We have to keep paddling to stay afloat, and our legs brush, and I want nothing more than to be inside of her right now.

Who the hell am I to say no?

"Yeah," I say. "Okay."

She bites her lip against a smile. "See you later, stud," she says. Then she dips underneath the surface of the water, vanishing into the inky dark.

My heart pounds in my chest. I feel her fingers on the

band of my shorts, and I shift awkwardly to help her get me out of them. The anticipation of her sweet mouth has me wound tight. I glance toward the flickering light of the bonfire to make sure no one's watching us—but no. They all seem occupied, snapping open fresh beers around the bonfire.

A couple of seconds pass, and the buzz of anticipation turns into a fizzle of fear. Did the riptide sweep her out?

But then I see her—a dark figure rising from the water. She emerges on the shore, climbing to her feet.

And she has my swim shorts in her hand.

My heart sinks like a stone in the deep.

I watch as she gets on shore, stands, and then turns back to me. Her fingers curl in a wave.

I groan. "Fuck—"

DONOVAN

Kenzi and I can't stop laughing as we make our escape.

"You're the worst," I tell her as I drive the golf cart back.

"Aw." Kenzi rakes her fingers through my hair. "You're the worst, too."

Jason's trunks flap in the wind, hanging off the golf cart antenna as we drive back to the marina.

It's going to be a long, naked walk back home for Jason King.

DONOVAN

Jason—the considerate guy—has a six-pack in the back of his golf cart.

We celebrate our win by splitting a beer between us. We sneak into the TV room, which is…exactly as a it sounds. A room with a TV and a couch. It's attached to the dock master's office, and it comes in handy for the boat owners who don't have cable.

I give Kenzi the remote, and she settles on VH1. The music videos provide good background noise as I make her unfold her prank in full detail.

"I've got to hand it to you," I tell her, "you've got a devious streak."

She cackles and takes a swig from the bottle. "That's me. Miss Horrible."

I shake my head. "I can't believe he bought it."

"I'm pretty sure he's accustomed to women throwing themselves at his feet."

I screw the corner of my mouth. "You've got that right. He thinks he's going to have sex with you."

She blinks at me. "What?"

"He said…" And I clear my throat now for a dramatic

retelling, and point ahead, my voice a growl. "That girl there. I'm going to fuck her this summer."

Kenzi screws up her nose. "Gross. Like he's going to throw me over his shoulder, caveman-style, and take me to his cave?"

"He probably has a shag-cave. Where susceptible women get the all-encompassing honor to getting screwed by Jason King."

Kenzi chuckles and puts her bottle to her lips, but her eyes stare into the far-off.

I call her out. "You're thinking about it, aren't you?"

"I'm…not!" she huffs, but she pulls a bit of hair behind her ear when she says it. She does add, "I guess there *are* worse ways to lose my virginity."

"No. There aren't. That's the absolute worst way. You don't want to be a notch on someone's flip-flops."

She shrugs. "Honestly, I'd *rather* be a notch. I can't think of anything worse than a rose-petal bed."

"Chilled champagne."

"Chocolate-covered strawberries on the pillow."

"Your lover playing an acoustic guitar softly from the bathtub."

We both look at each other and cackle.

"You're right. That does sound terrible."

Kenzi drops her head against the couch. Her raven hair drips over the back like a waterfall. "What was your first time like?"

"What, you mean besides the rose petals?"

She sticks out her tongue.

I steal the beer, take a swig, and then set it in my lap, loosely cradling the neck between both hands. "Miles Kronfeld," I tell her. "Seventh grade. His parents made him keep the bedroom door open at all times—boys or girls, didn't matter—which, in retrospect, was pretty forward of them, I guess. We'd have sleepovers, and one night he climbed into my bunk. We touched each other, and I'd just…watch the changes in his face. Listen to the hitch of his breath."

"So it was like…only handjobs? You two never…?" Kenzi extends her two pointer fingers and taps the tips together.

I frown. "What…because it wasn't penetrative, it doesn't count? It was intimate. Probably more intimate than most of the penetrative sex I've had. So, yeah. I count it."

"That's fair," Kenzi agrees. Her eyes drift to VH1, but I can tell she's not really watching. "Why does sex have to be so complicated?"

I shrug. "It doesn't."

"It's *my* body," Kenzi protests.

"It is."

"And I can do whatever I want with it."

I look her straight in those emerald eyes. "So what do you want to do with it?"

I'm not immune to the shift in the air between us. For a minute, it hangs. It's the feeling of putting on clothes straight out of the dryer—static electricity that makes your hair stand on end.

And then Kenzi leans in, and I lean in. We crash somewhere in the middle, mouth finding mouth, hands groping, feeling for…*something*. Like finding each other in the dark. We are sloppy. We are rushed. She tastes like cheap beer and fruity lip balm. I want to suck it off her lips.

The beer spills. No one cares. Our teeth click in our haste, and we chuckle about it, her warm breath a puff on my cheek. My lips find her neck. That sensitive spot underneath her ear. She moans and the sound plucks a cord inside of me that sends me trembling.

My mouth finds hers again, and this time, we taste each other. She licks the inside of my mouth, kitten-like. When we break apart, she sucks my bottom lip in her mouth and nibbles the steel of my lip ring.

There is something simultaneously so eager to please and

so innocent about her, and it goes straight to my groin. I could cut through diamonds right now.

I fall on top of her, pinning her to the couch. She grips my hair. She tugs at my shirt, and her legs wrap tightly around my waist, boa constrictor–style. Our hips wedge together, and we roll around, soaking in each other's heat. She lifts her arms, and I acquiesce and push her shirt and her bikini top over her head—they're both still damp, and they roll up together in a tangled mess before hitting the floor.

Her breasts spill out—beautiful, soft, and full—and she pulls my shirt off, and our skin feels so hot together, so *good* pressed together. I feel every brush of her fingertips. The warmth of every soft sigh. The movement of her body, undulating and jerking restlessly and wantingly underneath me.

It's almost too much. "Slow down," I try to coax her.

But she's animal-frantic, grabbing at me. "I want you inside of me," she pleads, her voice this low, heated thing.

"Yeah…" Mine, a gravelly growl that I barely recognize.

Her lips crush against mine, and I trip and fall into her kiss. There is a whole summer's worth of pent-up energy in me, and it zeros around every swipe of her tongue. The dark heat of her mouth. The way she tastes me, so curiously, so hungrily, as though she wants to trace every strand of my DNA with the tip of her tongue.

I am a line on a ship, wrapped around a winch, pulling tighter and tighter and tauter and tauter, until it trembles with the pressure, one more twist all it needs to make the whole thing snap apart—

"*Fuck!*" This is not a toe-curling moan of pleasure. This is the humiliated groan of a boy wound so tight, he comes apart.

In his pants. In his *fucking pants*.

I freeze on top of her.

Kenzi's breath patters against my lips, her silence unsure.

Still clinging to me. Then, timidly, she asks, "Did you just...uh...?"

"Yeah...*ugh*." I climb off her and sit up, retreating to my side of the couch. There's a decorative throw pillow in the opposite chair, and I snatch it up, hugging it in my lap. Hiding the shame stain.

"I swear, this has never happened to me before," I mutter into the seam of the pillow. "Is this like a...straight person thing? Because it sucks."

Kenzi sits up and runs her nails over the back of my neck. "Firsts for both of us, then."

"This was *not* your first time," I protest.

"You said it yourself—your first time doesn't have to be penetrative to count."

"Oh my God...do *not*. Do not repeat my idiot words back to me." I bury my face in the pillow. I feel sticky and sullied and ridiculous. "I wish I was Pinocchio."

"Because he's...made of wood?"

"No. Because he got swallowed up in the belly of a whale."

A light chuckle escapes Kenzi. "C'mon. It's not that bad. It's kind of flattering, actually."

"Great," I groan. "I'm going to go lie underneath a car now."

"*Stop*. You're so dramatic." She rests her chin on my shoulder. Her breath tickles my neck lightly, and eventually, it draws me out of my turtle shell. I roll out of my hunch and lift my head.

"Can we just...go back to being friends and pretend this part of the night never happened?"

She blinks at me, those green doe eyes all innocent. "Pretend *what* never happened?"

The silence between us is like steel wool against the skin. I want to say something, but all my words have jumped down my throat and refuse to resurface.

"I like this song," Kenzi says after a moment. "Turn it up?"

I do. We both stare at the video without really watching it. Halfway through, she gets close and rests her head on my shoulder.

"You're my best friend," she says after a minute, "You know that, right?"

"You're mine."

We're okay. We're going to be okay.

We stay up late, watching videos, just existing in each other's shared space.

9

———

KENZI

I'd love to rub my prank in Jason King's smug face.
But I can't.

Because he doesn't show up at the *Healing Touch* after that.

Which should be nice—no loud music playing all night, no constant cheering, as though we're docked next to a football stadium.

But it's not nice. It's boring. I find myself sitting on the bow of *Sweet Serenity* staring mournfully at the uninhabited cockpit, almost—

—No, don't say it—

Well, I almost *miss* the guy. Complete with his six-pack abs and arrogant smile.

Even Donovan and I are running out of things to talk about when we can't complain about Jason and his Merry Band of Jerks.

I'm starting to get that sinking feeling in my stomach… like maybe I went too far at the beach. I have a bad habit of not knowing when to draw the line. In trying to out-jerk the jerk…have I become the jerkiest of them all?

Ugh. The thought keeps me up at night more than I'd like to admit.

It's been about a week, not that I'm counting, since I've seen hide or hair or cocky grin from Jason King.

As if to compound the problem—karma kicks me in the ass.

"We're going on a sailing trip!" Pearl explains over breakfast at the Blue Heron—they do brunch specials for boaters. "Isn't that exciting?"

I break the yoke on my Croque Madame. "Huh?"

"Three nights on the old blue," Four says, grinning. "Just you, me, your mom, and the stars. Doesn't that sound nice?"

Double ugh.

The only thing worse than being without Jason is being without Donovan.

"It's only three nights," he says when I tell him, feeling close to crying for no reason at all. "I think you'll live."

I don't *feel* like I'm going to live, though. I pout even as Donovan and his dad cast us off, *Sweet Serenity*'s motor purring.

"Heads up," Donovan says as he unhooks the rope from the cleat and tosses it my way. I catch it.

We're officially cast off, ready to leave the marina.

Donovan, however, grabs the siding before we can get too far. "Hey, Kenzi. For the road."

He reaches into his back pocket, pulls something out, and hands it over.

It's a flat CD case. Inside, a CD with Sharpie written on it. "For Kenzi."

A mixed tape. Donovan made me a mixed tape.

I bite my lip to keep my smile from overwhelming my face. "Thanks, bud."

"You're welcome, bud." He releases the side, and the boat chugs out of the slip, leaving Donovan standing on the pier. His form gets smaller, but it's still there as Four steers us out of the mouth of the harbor and into the open waters.

I slip on my headphones. The boat vibrates underneath me, the engine making the whole thing hum. There's a folded-up piece of paper in the CD case, where Donovan listed all the songs and bands. The first song is by a band called the Pixies, and immediately, their dark, chaotic sounds sweep me away. It's all *very Donovan*, and I close my eyes to enjoy it.

We're sailing up Long Island to Block Island. It's about a five-hour trip by sailboat, give or take, depending on the "knots," says Four. Four comes out, takes off the sail cover, and hoists the sail up. I help him a bit, but I'm pretty sure it's just his attempt to "bond" with me. Besides, Pearl is far too busy downing daiquiris in the cockpit.

Pearl makes guacamole, and we munch on chips as we sail. Sailing, like fishing, swimming, and everything else in the water, is slow and tedious. All about the *journey*, not the destination, blah, blah, blah.

I listen to Donovan's CD twice, read a few chapters, and play about twenty hands of blackjack with Pearl and Four. Four even lets me take the helm, which is, admittedly, more fun than I expected.

I feel so short behind the huge wheel, but he points to a small blinking green dot ahead. "Just make sure to keep that on your left," he tells me. "Otherwise, we'll end up in the rocks."

No pressure.

Just as I'm starting to get the hang of it, I hear a howling behind me. I glance over and see it—

In the middle of this calm, glass-sea day…a roaring monster.

The *Healing Touch* speeds through, slicing through the serenity. The motorboat flies passed us, bouncing along.

As they go by, I can see the passengers: the King family.

Mrs. King is sunbathing on the bow—the forty-year-old has a body that even I am jealous of. Mr. King is at the helm. And then there's Jason. In his polo. He's hanging his long limbs over the edge of the boat, looking bored. But when he sees me, he smiles. For me.

Cue my stomach, clenching.

And, just like that, they're gone.

"Hold on!" Four says.

At first, I don't know why, and then it hits—the *Healing Touch* is followed up by a series of wakes, and they roll through the water, shaking our boat back and forth.

* * *

Hour nine of complete confinement with Four and Pearl.

We finally made it to Block Island, and now we're attached to a mooring ball. A single boat bobbing in a small lake of boats.

Pearl is taking a midday nap to avoid a hangover later. Four is playing solitaire.

I entertain myself by sitting in the cockpit and painting my toenails. Seashell pink.

I'm touching up my big toe when Jason's face breaks through the water.

I screech. My polish goes everywhere.

Jason clings to the stairs. His hair is darker when wet. Salt water drips down his chest, making the muscles glisten.

"Hey, Trouble," he says. He blinks water from his eyelashes. Have I noticed before how long they are?

"Jesus! Are you a mermaid?"

"Maybe." He's grinning again—that cocky smirk. "Dad wanted to invite your family over for dinner tonight. We're grilling steaks."

I'm trying to ignore the way the water sparkles on his broad shoulders. The droplets slipping down his biceps.

"Okay," I say. "I'll pass on the word, I guess."

"Good. We're on Moor 16."

A loud whistle cuts through the air, and Jason glances over his shoulder.

"Is that for you?" I ask.

"Dad is timing my swim," he responds. He looks back at me, his eyes sweeping. "I'll see you tonight."

"Maybe."

"Do better than maybe." He winks and then pushes off the side of the boat. He moves through the water effortlessly, his arms swinging up and over.

I'm not ashamed to admit I watch the muscles of his back flex as he glides through the water.

Okay. Maybe a little ashamed.

What's gotten into me?

* * *

Pearl fits me into a purple blouse and white pants—which seems like a stupid idea, ultimately, because my butt gets wet as soon as we get in the dingy.

Four steers us through the water and to the *Healing Touch*. The boat has its own *underneath boat* lights, and they make the water look emerald green in their spotlights.

"Ahoy there!" Four says, like the nerd he is.

"Terry," Mr. King smiles. "Glad to have you. I'll toss you a line."

We tie up to their boat. Mr. King extends a hand and helps us all on board, one by one.

It's funny—it doesn't feel like the same boat with the rest of the King family here. I'm used to seeing this as the party boat. Now, I see it as it's supposed to be. The wings of the center console have fanned out into a long table. There's soft jazz music playing, not the normal rancorous pop tunes. The table is set, a bottle of wine in the middle, flanked with salad, bread, and steak and potatoes.

It's amazing how the *Healing Touch* cleans up when it's not covered in wine coolers and slutty teenagers.

Pearl and Mrs. King get along like gangbusters. They're both gold diggers, wear the same brand of jewelry, and ascribe to the same skincare routine. It stands to reason. The grill is attached to the back of the boat, and Mr. King and Four hover over it, talking about…meat and fishing, I guess. Guy stuff.

Jason's brother, Ian, is at the bow of the boat. Every now and then, a gust blows the smell of clove cigarettes our way.

Jason himself is dressed in a nice white button-up. Tan slacks. We sit side by side, and his arm hair tickles my skin.

"Should I keep an eye on you?" he asks.

"Why?"

"Every time you're around, bad things happen to me."

"Then, yes. You should definitely keep an eye on me."

His dad announces that dinner is ready, which is good. It's bad for me to have Jason King this close, smelling like patchouli and salt water. It gives me a bad urge to lick him from his collarbone, up his Adam's apple, to his plump bottom lip.

God, I need to lose my virginity. Like, *now*. This repression is no good for anyone.

I take it out on my steak. I cut into it like Jack the Ripper. It's cooked perfectly—just a little on the rare side. I try to focus on the meat on my plate, instead of the *man meat* sitting beside me.

Jason is different around his family, though. Like the boat, he's cleaned up. Hair slicked back. Eyes bright and alert. I've known him as the party animal, but here, under his dad's eye, the boy might as well have a halo over his head. He's *that* much of a good boy.

"I feel like I haven't seen you around lately, Jason," Four

says as he cuts into his steak.

Realizing I've tuned out, I tune back in.

"He's grounded," says Ian—which is the first time I've heard him speak all night. He has a particularly joyful glint in his eyes when he says it, and I get the impression it's a rarity even in the confines of his own house for Jason King to suffer the consequences of his actions, and Ian is gloating about it.

"There was an incident at the marina," Mr. King expounds. "Jason, why don't you tell us about it?"

"He got the boat stuck on a sandbank," Ian snickers.

Mr. King glances sideways at Ian. "Is your name Jason?"

Ian drops his eyes. "No, sir."

I freeze midchew, the meat half-masticated in my mouth. My eyes lock on Jason, waiting for the sharp sting of just revenge. Four and Pearl know nothing about the prank Donovan and I played, and I guess it's due time I got drawn and quartered for it on the dinner table.

Jason's blue eyes sweep to me—a parting *got ya*? But then he does something strange.

He shrugs and turns back to his plate. "I tried to take it out at night. My bad."

Is he…taking the blame?

I'm shocked. I didn't think Jason King had a martyr bone in his body, but here he is. Taking the rap and doing time—in his dad's mansion, but *still*—for my crime.

Why would he let us off the hook like that?

I swallow my bite of steak. The lump feels weird in my throat.

"Listen to this boy—*my bad*," Mr. King repeats, a smile playing softly on his lips. "It tore up the bottom of the boat. We had to have it resanded." He points his fork to the sky. "Do you hear that?"

"Hear what?" Pearl asks.

Mr. King takes out a small remote from his pocket and

presses a button. The music gets louder. "The popping in the stereo."

I can *barely* hear it, but if I strain, every five seconds, there's a small *pop* of air in the beats.

"Music blasted too loud wears and tears on the system…" He turns the music down again. "Kids have no respect for the power of the tools they wield."

Jason shrugs. "Sorry."

"I remember when I was a teenager," Four says with a chuckle, "Couldn't blast my music loud enough! It's why I can't hear a damn thing anymore."

Mr. King doesn't seem to hear Four, though. He's staring directly at his son. "Jason," he says smoothly, "would you like to try that again?"

Jason's hands stop moving. The table lapses into a silence, except for the small clatter of forks and knives moving.

"What?" he asks.

Mr. King's fingers lace together. "Your apology. Would you like to try that again?" He smiles, but the nice mask of his face doesn't match the intensity of his words. "With meaning, this time."

I don't understand what he's asking for, but Jason's expression sobers completely, like he's been hit with a pail of ice water. Slowly, he puts his utensils down. He rises to his feet and puts his palms flat on the table, like something practiced.

"My actions were irresponsible and immature," he recites to the table. "And they've ruined the ambiance of this dinner. Please accept my apology."

My breath is caught in my throat, and I can't look at Jason. The secondhand embarrassment is unreal. Mr. King may as well have put him over his lap and spanked him in front of all of us—*that's* how embarrassing this feels.

I want to say something to let him off the hook, but my words are stuck in my throat. And, honestly, I'm *afraid* of Mr.

King in this moment. I'm afraid of drawing his wrath, afraid of saying the wrong thing and being forced to put on some self-debasing performance in the same way. After all, who am I? Just a stranger on his boat. Jason is his *son*—by the look of it, his favorite son—and even he doesn't get an inch of mercy from the man.

The tension is ugly, and, for once, I'm grateful for Four's lack of tact, because he's the only one who doesn't seem to get how awkward this is. "What's that, boy?" he jokes. "You'll have to say that into my good ear." Then he laughs. "I'm only fooling! These ears, though, not what they used to be."

Pearl forces a laugh. "Terry, you're incorrigible." The Kings offer obligatory chuckles of their own.

Jason, however, doesn't move. I can see his arms still braced beside me, locked in position, unwavering. I don't know if he's even breathing at this point.

Finally, Mr. King releases him with an "Apology accepted."

Jason drops his arms and returns to his seat. He goes back to his food, but he doesn't say another word at dinner after that. His hand is stuck a fist, and it doesn't unclench.

Conversation returns. Every now and then, someone will direct a sentence Jason's way, and he'll offer a smile. But I've seen Jason King smile. His smiles come with a healthy dose of arrogance and mischief, dimples in his cheeks, a twinkle of danger in his eyes.

This smile has none of that. His face is a mannequin, empty. His body is here, but his soul has left the dinner table for the night.

Conversation moves listlessly from one topic to the next, like a paper boat bopping in the water. I lapse in and out of focus, but I'm finding it hard to concentrate. Jason King took the rap for me. And he took it *hard.* But why?

When we finish up dinner, Jason finally speaks. "Is everyone finished? Can I clear the table?"

"Yes," Pearl says with a sweep of her hand. "That's very kind of you, thank you."

I don't think it has anything to do with him being kind, though—I get the feeling he just wants to exit as quickly as possible, and I can't blame him for that.

He stands and picks up his plate. He touches mine. "Can I take your plate?"

I grip it. "I'll help."

Together, we clear the table. Jason and I go downstairs, into the belly of the *Healing Touch*. We dump the dishes in the sink.

"I'll wash, you dry?" Jason offers.

"Works for me."

We find a rhythm—he suds and scrubs, and I dry everything off with a towel before putting it on the dish rack.

"So," I start. "You didn't tell your dad that I cast off your boat?"

"Nope."

"Why not?"

"Dad's version of *grounded* is making me do laps in the pool and play table tennis. I think I'll live."

"He seems a little stricter than that," I offer.

He shrugs. "I guess."

He doesn't want to talk about it, and I can't blame him. So I counter with "Besides, I didn't think self-sacrifice was really your style."

"Isn't it?" He casts me a curious side-eye. "What's my style?"

"Spoiled rich boy who sneaks by on his good looks and Daddy's money."

"So you think I'm good-looking?"

I feel my face go hot. I hand a dish back. "You missed a spot."

He chuckles as he rewashes a perfectly clean plate.

"What's your deal?" I ask.

"What do you mean?"

"Like…what do you want to do with your life?"

"I'm going to become a doctor."

"Like father, like son?"

"Something like that."

"Do you want to work at the hospital?"

His jaw tightens. He doesn't move his eyes from his plate. "You're going to laugh at me."

"Maybe. But I'll wait until you're out of earshot."

He casts me a sidelong look. Finally, he says, "I want to join the Peace Corps."

He's right. That catches me completely off guard.

Jason King is full of surprises tonight.

"Why?" I ask.

He glances at me. "Isn't it obvious? You tell a girl you spent a year in the Peace Corps—instant panty-dropper."

I roll my eyes. *That's* a little more his style…but I can tell he doesn't mean it.

"Okay…besides panty-dropping. Why else?" I ask.

"And…I don't know." He shrugs. He turns his focus back on the plates, works on soaping and scrubbing. "I've had a good life. I guess I just…want to give something back. Make a difference."

The way he says it…it's like it's something shameful. Like his heart of gold is something that is meant to be hidden away underneath his bed, behind his porn collection.

"So why don't you?"

"My dad says if I want to do something good, I should do what he does. Make millions and donate to a good cause."

I shrug. "That's one way to do it, sure. But is that what you want?"

"I don't know."

I scoff. "I don't buy it."

He narrows his eyes at me. "What?"

"If you want to join…just do it. Screw your dad. You're

Jason King. You get everything you want."

He doesn't take his eyes away from me. "Not everything."

I let out a light laugh. My turn to examine my plate. "Wow. Are you really hitting on me over the sink?"

"Well, you are already wet..."

He closes his fist and opens it fast, flicking water at me. I yelp and put my hand on his chest, giving him a shove. "Dick!"

He's so solid, has so much muscle mass, that my shove barely makes him sway.

It suddenly occurs to me that my hand is still on his chest —hard and full of muscles—and like this, we're close. I don't move away. Neither does he.

"I like you," he confesses suddenly. It sounds simple the way he says it, yet I feel like the floor has been yanked from under me, and I'm floundering in the water below.

"Why?"

"You're different."

"Different? Fat? Nerdy? You're going to have to be more specific."

"You don't let anyone tell you what to do. You're the only one who calls me on my shit."

"Someone has to."

We're close, now. Close enough to kiss.

I imagine the warmth of his lips. Would they taste like salt water?

I think about Donovan. And a stone rolls over my heart.

I can't. He's my only friend here...and he'd kill me if he knew I was making out with the enemy.

A clattering of laughter from the deck jerks me back to reality. I step back, putting some space between us. Like that, the moment shatters.

"We should...go back up," I say. My heart is pounding in my chest.

"You go," he says. "I'll finish up."

I want to argue, but I'm afraid if I spend any more time down here with him, I won't be able to stop myself from letting Jason King pin me to the sink and soak me.

I climb above deck. It's cooler out here. The fresh air feels good on my hot cheeks. Anchored out in the middle of the lake...I finally start to understand this *living on the water* thing.

I haven't seen so many stars in my entire life. They dot the sky like glitter. The light from the moon echoes across the still, black water. A satellite blinks across the sky. I can see it as clearly as if I had a telescope.

There's a lantern on deck that illuminates the guests. Pearl, Four, and Mrs. King are chatting. The ember from Ian's cigarette glows on and off again from the bow.

Mr. King hangs off the back of the boat. He's taken the mesh from the grill, and he's scraping it clean over the side.

I walk over to him and sit down on the bench beside him.

"Can I help?" I ask.

He glances up at me. They both have it—that arrogant, boyish smirk. Mr. King, I'm sure, was attractive in his time. He's good-looking now, even, if you're into the silver fox thing.

Jason King will grow up attractive, which bodes well for my fantasies of growing old with him, 2.5 kids that look just like us running around our feet...

Snap out of it!

Mr. King points to a soap bottle. "Hand me that?"

I do. He squirts the soap over the grill. "Is this your first time?"

"Sorry?"

"On the ocean."

"Oh. I guess."

"I wouldn't trade it for anything. You won't find peace like this anywhere else." He looks over at me. "What is it you want to do with your life, Kenzi?"

An intense question, but. Sure. "I'd like to do something with music."

"Make it?"

"Produce it."

A smile crawl over his mouth. "Good girl. I know there was an ambitious woman in there somewhere."

"Thanks."

"Jason seems fond of you."

He does? "I guess."

"Enjoy it. Summer fun. I had it in my heyday, too." His hand meets my shoulder then, and he squeezes. "Just don't forget what it is. Fun. Don't let anything come between you and your dreams."

Geez, this isn't the conversation I was expecting. I don't know what I expected. But I certainly didn't think Jason's dad was going to lecture me on the pitfalls of falling in love.

I've got Pearl for that. What is it about getting old that makes people so jaded?

"Mr. King?" I squeak out.

"Yes?"

"I was the one who set your boat loose. It floated off the dock and hit the shore. It was a dumb prank. It wasn't Jason."

There's a change in his eyes. A flicker. I can't tell if he's pissed...or impressed. Maybe both? He nods once, and his hand drops from my shoulder. "I see."

That's all he says. Then there's silence. It's scary, his silence. I feel my stomach flatten. Did I do the right thing? Jason might no longer be grounded...but what if I got Pearl and Four in trouble instead?

I imagine them standing at the end of the dock with a megaphone, confessing to the marina: *I apologize for having a terrible daughter. It was wrong of me.*

"I'll do whatever you want," I quickly blurt out. "I'll clean your boat or do chores or..."

"Do you think I'm harsh, Kenzi?" he asks, which catches

me off guard, so I say nothing. "You went quiet at dinner," he continues. "I imagine you thought I was being cruel and unusual to Jason. Do you have any brothers?"

"No," I say.

"Boys," he says, "are different to raise from girls. Girls, you have to encourage them. Build their spine. Boys have to be taught respect. Disciplined. Trouble has to be broken. Otherwise, they'll run wild."

What the hell am I supposed to say to *that*? "I don't know about that," I say.

He arches an eyebrow and smiles, as though pleased at the challenge. "No?"

"Girls can be wild, too."

He laughs—it's startling, a low chuckle from his belly. "Yes," he says. "I suppose they can be. You're not pregnant, are you?"

"Um…no."

"Good girl." He smiles now, but somehow it's not a comforting smile. He gives my shoulder a strong squeeze. "Let me know if that changes. We can work something out."

I want to die on the spot. Is this how rich people talk? Self-debasement and abortions before dessert? What planet are they from?

My mother materializes, as if she can sense my discomfort. I feel like I need her right now; I'm a child with my hand in the lion's mouth.

She plays with a strand of my hair. "How're you doing, ducky?"

"Tired," I say, feeling very small.

"I know," she murmurs, her long nails brushing my forehead. "We'll head home soon."

"Your daughter has guts, Mrs. Stratton." He winks at me, like we share some scandalous secret, and I retreat tighter against my mother. "Make sure she doesn't lose them."

KENZI

Falling asleep, it turns out, is going to be a task.

The boat isn't huge. Even with my door closed, I can still hear Four and my mom knocking around in their bedroom. They've both had too much wine, and it makes Pearl's laughter pitchy.

I groan and bunch up my pillow around my head to try to block out the sounds. No luck.

Then I remember—bingo. My Walkman is tucked into the wooden shelf that holds my belongings. I pluck it out and open the player, popping Donovan's mix in it. Then I slip my headphones over my ears, flop onto my back, and press Play.

Immediately, hard smashing drums and wild guitar riffs blow my ear drums. Smashing Pumpkins. Tool. The Pixies. If Donovan were a sound, this CD would be it. Angry and cynical, but beautiful, too. I'm surprised there's no My Chemical Romance, but I guess that's too "mainstream" for him. Donovan always has to be slightly left of the beaten path. The sounds are like a bruise, blue, purple, with streaks of sunset red. The familiarity of it is comforting, even if the noise is raucous and chaotic, and I close my eyes to it.

The track changes. The bass is low and heavy. The beat of

the drum matches my own pulse. The singer's voice is dark and obsessive.

I feel my mind drift. I imagine I'm back in the belly of the *Healing Touch*. The dishes are piled up in the sink. Only this time, we let them sit. Jason's tall frame traps me between himself and the kitchen counter. Those impossibly blue eyes don't leave my gaze. His hand goes to the side of my face, but I don't pull away. I let him trace his thumb over my bottom lip.

"Open," he says, and I part my lips.

He crooks his finger inside the warm cavern of my mouth. My eyes don't leave his, not once, not even as I suck the digits, sliding my tongue against his long fingers.

"You're beautiful," he tells me. "A beautiful, filthy girl."

In my fantasies, Jason is equal parts reverent and dirty. His removes his fingers from my mouth and pushes them underneath my dress. He dives his hand without flourish inside my panties and pushes his fingers against my slit, which is already dripping wet for him.

He makes a noise, like a laugh, and his Adam's apple bobs. "Is this for me?"

"Yes," I whimper.

"You are desperate," he sneers. He's teasing me. Belittling me.

And in the safety of my dark fantasies, I spread my legs for more.

"You're trouble," he says. "And trouble has to be broken."

When he pushes inside of me, he breaks me.

* * *

Are you broken? Are you broken, Kenzi?

* * *

"Kenzi."

My father's voice. The car stalled, engine growling.

His black eyes. His hand outstretched. "Get in the car."

I don't want to. His breath, his clothes, his whole car smells like liquor. Like someone opened up a bottle of scotch and just dumped it over the seats. There are spiderwebs of red veins around his eyes. He hasn't shaved in days, and his beard is uneven, patchy.

The passenger-side door is open, but I don't go toward it. I stand in the uncut front lawn of our house. I don't want to make these decisions. I'm just a six-year-old with a backpack.

"You love me, don't you, baby?"

I nod. My voice is stuck in my throat.

"Then get in."

I don't know what else to do. I start to walk forward—

"Kenzi!" My mother's voice now, a wail behind me that stops me in my tracks. She grabs my backpack, pulls me backward, and launches herself forward toward the car. They talk for a minute—angry, rapid adult voices that blur in my ears. Then he calls her a sharp word and slams the door shut.

"Don't do this!" she shouts. "I love you, John! I love you!"

But his wheels scream on the asphalt, and the car takes off. My mother gets halfway down the road before she stops chasing him.

That's the last time I see my father. His car will slide off the road that night, killing him and injuring two others.

My mother collapses on the lawn and cries. Her *I love yous* haunt me, even now.

This is what love is, says the primordial ooze of my six-year-old brain.

Love is what a man bribes you with to get you into his death-car.

Love is the strongest woman I know, brought to her knees, helpless and wailing.

Love is a child, alone, scared.

This is what love is, and I don't want any part of it.

My tiny fingers turn to fists. I dig my nails into my palm.

"Wake up," I say, gritting my teeth. *"Wake up."*

* * *

My breath catches in my throat. My heart is pounding, my blood is screaming, and I blink at the low ceiling, the V-shaped walls, and struggle to remember where the hell I am.

I'm on a boat. In the ocean. My father is dead, and he can't get me here.

My hands have fisted in my sleep. Slowly, I unclench them.

I'm still trying to breath, still trying to slow the adrenaline rush coursing in my veins, when there's a soft knock on the door.

"Kenzi?" Pearl opens the door and steps inside. Her hair is pinned up to her skull, and she's wearing a silk robe.

I still have the headphones half twisted around my head, and I untangle them and shove the Walkman to the side.

Her eyebrows knit as she looks at me. "Are you alright?"

I nod. My tongue feels thick, and it's hard to peel it from the roof of my mouth. "Sorry," I say, "was I…making noises?"

I shout in my sleep, sometimes. But she shakes her head. "No. I just…had a strange feeling that you needed me."

My heart gets tight in my chest, but I say nothing.

She motions to the bed. "Room for one more?"

"Yeah."

I scoot over. Pearl slides into bed with me and puts her arm around my middle.

"It's us against the world, darling," she murmurs.

She smells like wax and coconut oil. I feel suddenly exhausted, like I've just come back from the trenches of war. I pass out in her arms, against the rise and fall of her chest.

DONOVAN

Kenzi is gone for a total of four days, three nights, and six hours.

But who's counting?

I'm standing at the tip of the finger pier when *Sweet Serenity* makes her slow turn into the neck of the marina.

The boat purrs around into the slip, Terry at the helm. Kenzi is stretched out on the bow like a cat, sitting on a towel, headphones hanging around her neck. Her legs are incredibly long underneath her cut-off jeans, and she has her shirt tied in a knot underneath her breasts, exposing her soft belly. Her oversized sunglasses turn my way, and she smiles.

She's such a sight for sore eyes, it makes me ache.

The boat pulls into the slip. She comes to the side, and I toss her a rope.

"Missed me?" she asks.

"You wish."

The engine hasn't even cut, but she jumps from the boat to the pier, and we take off down the dock.

* * *

Smoke fills my lungs and fills my skull.

I close my eyes and drop my head against the wall.

I feel hazy, quiet, relaxed. All my tense, tight muscles gain some slack.

Someone's laundry tumbles and thumps in the machine beside mine. The laundry room smells like Clorox, handfuls of earth, and weed. People so rarely come in here, Kenzi and I have claimed this spot for our intermediate smoke breaks.

"Maybe we might've judged Jason too harshly," Kenzi says suddenly.

I open my eyes just enough to narrow them at her. "What?"

She shrugs. She's twisting the joint between her fingers, examining the glowing cherry. "I'm just saying…maybe he's not the *complete* dick we thought he was."

"So he's just a small dick. That's what you're saying?"

The edges of Kenzi's mouth twist in a grimace. She looks away.

My throat, already smoke-swollen, fills with acid.

"Jesus Christ," I say. "You fell for it. His charm."

"I did not." She looks at me now. Those sea-glass-green eyes look equal parts angered and hurt.

The mood is broken. There's a tension in the toxic air between us.

"Why are you defending him?" I counter. "He hates people like us. We're not worth licking the dirt on his shoes, according to him."

"And what exactly is that? *People like us?*"

Her eyes are challenging me.

Like an idiot, I meet the challenge. "Losers."

A shard of hurt slips across her eyes. "Is that what you think of me?"

I lift a hand, drop it. "That's what *they* think of us. Jason and his crew."

She pushes herself off the dryer and brushes off her dress.

"That's funny, because *Jason* never called me a loser. But you did."

I jump off and follow her down the gravel pathway to the dock. "Kenzi, that's not what I meant..."

She turns to me suddenly. "Is that why you...?" But her question catches, and her voice trails off.

My throat lumps. How do I tell her now that it's not that I don't want her...

The problem is *wanting her too much*? The type of longing that makes your soul ache.

My words go brittle and crack. "Kenzi..."

She shakes her head. "Just leave me alone for a minute. Please."

Please. When she says please, I can't do anything but obey.

My feet are trapped to the ground like they're stuck in tar, and I watch her walk down the dock and away from me.

* * *

I don't see Kenzi for a couple of days.

It feels like a lifetime.

I'm not sure if she's still mad at me about the loser comment. I spend nearly a full twenty-four hours downloading music off Limewire and burning it onto a CD. I put it in a case, climb onto her boat, and leave it trapped in the hatch window that leads to her room.

But the next day, the CD is still there. She hasn't come back to the boat.

I'm trying not to let it consume me. But it's a challenge. I find myself spending too much time staring off into the void blankly.

"Donovan." I glance up from my notebook. I've been distractedly doodling the letter *K* in the corner.

I've been zoning out during the Tomorrow's Doctors class. Dr. Esmerelda is staring at me expectantly from across

the conferences table. "Team up with Jason for the assign-
ment, please."

My chest gets tight. I look at Jason, but for once, he
doesn't have murder in his eyes.

Actually, he's been in a bizarrely good mood today. And I
feel like I'm walking on a minefield around him, waiting for
the bomb to detonate, because it can't be this easy.

The class dives into teams of two. Each team is given a
stethoscope and a blood pressure cuff. Our task is to accu-
rately take the pulse and pressure of our partner.

Simple enough, at least. Jason goes first. I have to roll up
my sleeve so he can take my blood pressure. This is easy
for him.

He jots down my statistics in his notebook. Then he rolls
up his sleeves and extends his arm. He's distracted, though.
He keeps glancing off into nothing, getting lost in his
thoughts.

"This is familiar," I say, trying to draw him back to reality.

For the first time, his blue eyes meet mine. "What?"

"Come on. You don't remember?" He looks at me blankly,
so I continue. "Four summers ago. I was practicing to get my
lifeguard certificate so I could pull a couple shifts at the pool.
You volunteered to be my CPR dummy and then complained
that I nearly broke your ribs."

Jason looks startled. "I forgot about that."

"I didn't," I say. "You weren't always an asshole."

He grins. "But always a dummy."

I bite back a smile of my own. "Won't argue there."

I count his blood pressure and then remove the sleeve.
Then I attach the stethoscope. He's wearing a white knitted
sweater, and it's going to be hard to hear anything through
that. "Can you take off your sweater?" I ask.

He answers by lifting his sweater an inch. Nothing but
bare skin underneath.

"Do you mind if I go underneath?"

"Go wild."

I cup the stethoscope and rub it between my hands. "What are you doing?" he asks.

"It's cold."

Jason snorts a laugh, but he doesn't say anything else.

Once I've gotten the temperature of the stethoscope up a bit, I roll my chair directly in front of Jason. His limbs are too long, and he has to splay his knees to make room for me. I slip the stethoscope underneath his sweater. His skin is warm, and I hear him make a small intake of breath—the metal is still a little cold, despite my best intentions—but he otherwise doesn't complain.

I slide the tool up his chest and over his heart. I'm focused, zeroed in on the *whump-whump* beat.

It's strong. Loud. And thumping quickly against his chest.

"Are you nervous?" I ask him.

His mouth screws. "Why would I be nervous?"

"Your pulse is fast—"

I stop my tongue. It hits me then. We're so close like this. His heart is pounding. His pupils are dilated. His chest rises and falls in short, quick breaths.

Jason is *not* nervous. He's aroused.

I know. And he knows that I know. I can tell by the spike of fear in his eyes. But then they narrow. "You're doing it wrong," he mutters.

His heart is *hammering* in my ears.

I suggest, "Try taking a breath—"

But Jason suddenly rips the stethoscope from me and throws it across the room. "This exercise is stupid!" he snaps. "Twelve-year-olds can play with stethoscopes!"

"Jason!" Dr. Esmerelda is livid. Her eyes are sharp, her mouth a thin line. "Don't make me call your father down here, because you know I will. Outside. Now."

Jason doesn't look at me. He just snatches up his notebook and leaves, shutting the door hard behind him.

12

KENZI

I'm too busy to notice Jason the first time he tries to get my attention. I'm belly-down on the bow of the boat reading *Dracula* and finding that Donovan's mix provides the perfect background soundtrack to the erotic gothic classic.

Until over the edges of my pages, I see Jason's bright eyes, cocky grin. His mouth moves, and I tug my headphones off my ears with "What?"

"Sorry for the intrusion, ma'am," he says. He's holding a clipboard, which he taps with his pen. "I've come with official dock master business."

He's wearing a shirt so small, it shows off his midriff (which, I can't help but notice, is incredibly toned). It takes me a second to recognize the lighthouse logo at his chest—

I squint. "Is that Donovan's shirt?"

"It's come to my attention you haven't filled out the new boat-owner form."

I roll my eyes at his bizarre roleplay. "How long is this going to take?"

"Longer if you keep interrupting me. Now." He turns to the clipboard. "Your state of residence?"

69

"Jupiter."

He pretends to jot my answer down. "Current age?"

"Eighteen, going on eight hundred."

"Have you captained a boat before?"

"Once, but the pirates made me walk the plank when they realized I was a witch."

"I see." Scribble, scribble. "Do you have a boyfriend?"

I'm so surprised by that, the sound I make is a hiccupped noise: an incredulous half scoff, half laugh. "A...what?"

His eyes finally leave the clipboard and meet mine. Those blues are brighter than the sky itself. "Boyfriend, girlfriend, friend with benefits...?"

"I...no!" My face burns. I force my tongue to unknot and throw his question back at him. "What's it to you?"

That dangerous, crooked smile lifts the edge of his mouth. "Will you come get ice cream with me?"

I blink. I have to piece the words together, like a child learning to speak. "You're asking me out. To ice cream. *You.* Jason King."

He points his pen to himself. "Me, Jason King." Then he jabs the pen at me. "You, Kenzi Stratton."

He's such a dork, and no matter how hard I bite the inside of my cheek, I can't help the smile that creeps across my lips.

He lights up. "Is that a yes?"

I shake my head. "No!" I say, maybe more forceful than I should. "Absolutely no."

His smile drops. "What? Why not? You've got somewhere better to be?"

"*Literally* anywhere."

He opens his mouth to say something, but he's interrupted by a shout—"Hey!"

Donovan charges down the dock with a scowl. He's in a stained shirt and jeans with too many rips in them—he's clearly in the middle of laundry day. He snaps at Jason. "Give me my shirt back."

Jason takes a couple steps back, but he isn't retreating—he's grinning, like a cat playing with the mouse before it strikes. "What…is this shirt yours? I had no idea."

"Give. It. Back."

Jason takes off the shirt then and holds it out to Donovan.

"I was only borrowing it, dude," Jason says, as though they're friends now. "Chill."

Donovan's face is red. He snatches the shirt back.

Ugh. This got ugly quick.

"Hey, Jason," I say, "next time you want to go through someone's laundry, I've got a pair of panties that are your color."

Jason winks at me. "Take them off on our date and I'll consider it."

I wrinkle my nose at him. "There is no date."

"We'll see."

Jason exits, climbing on board the *Healing Touch*. I sigh and turn back to Donovan. "Are you okay—?"

But Donovan is already halfway up the dock, his back to me.

13

____

JASON

*I*t's 2:00 p.m. on a Tuesday and I'm already buzzed.

I lounge across the picnic table on the lawn, my legs hanging off the edge. The sun warms me, and I close my eyes.

Around me, I hear sounds of chatter—Amy and Brett, gossiping about the last episode of *Flavor of Love*. The boombox beats and clears out any chaos inside my skull.

I'm lazy. Warm. A lion, king of the jungle, sunning himself on Pride fucking Rock.

"Hey, King."

I squint my eyes open to see Nick coming down the gravel pathway from the shitty laundry room. The locals use it for—well, laundry, I guess. Everyone else uses it as a place to get high.

"Sup?"

"Check this out."

I peel myself up and hop off the table. I follow Nick into the laundry room, and he nods to the corkboard.

They've got notices pinned here—reminders of when and where to pay slip fees, someone's desperate attempt at a potluck. And something else: a note in girly handwriting that says, *For the laundry thief...I think these are yours?*

And pinned to the note, a pair of red, lacy women's panties.

I chuckle. *Well played, Kenzi.*

"You know what this is?" Nick asks.

"Yeah," I say. "It's a dare." Then I unpin the panties from the corkboard.

14

KENZI

*I*t's beach day for the Strattons. And Four.

We leave the boat and walk to the parking lot bogged down with beach chairs, umbrellas, and thermal bags.

Four and Pearl walk ahead side by side. Pearl, as a rule, only ever carries her purse. She has her arm linked together with Four's as they walk, and she laughs at his bad dad jokes.

Meanwhile, I hoof it with a beach chair strapped to my back and another heavy bag on my shoulder. The family camel.

"Hey, Kenzi!"

At the sound of my name, I stop and turn around (with no over-the-shoulder visibility, the chair on the back requires me to make a full turn). Jason and his crew are at the marina's swimming pool. When I see Jason, however, my jaw drops.

He's standing on one of the pool chairs, arms outstretched. He's all tall, lean muscle, each and every one of them on display. Because he's wearing nothing except for the bright red lacy panties that I pinned to the corkboard yesterday.

Holy cow. Leave it to Jason King to turn a prank into a fashion statement.

He drops off the chair and walks to the gate. I meet him on the other side of the gate, gawking. I hate that I can see the definition biceps. His abdomen. That dangerous V that slips down his hips.

He swaggers up to the gate, all cocky. "What do you think?"

I lift my eyebrows. "You know this is a family-friendly pool, right?"

Jason glances down and tugs at the lace. "What, are the boys showing?"

I follow his gaze and…Jesus Christ on a cracker. The panties really do *nothing* to contain the massive package trapped underneath.

My poor, pent-up hormones are no match for the sight, and I feel my insides clench.

"Well…I've got to hand it to you," I say, trying to play it cool. "You pull it off."

"You think?" He grins. "If you like them, I'll wear them to our date."

I roll my eyes. "Still not happening."

But he doesn't look defeated. Instead, that cocky smirk remains intact. "You're going to give in. Eventually. Just so you know."

"What, afraid of a challenge?"

"Clearly not."

My eyes haven't left his. Despite myself, I realize…*I'm enjoying this.* A lot. I like making Jason King work for my attention. I *like* Jason King *giving* me attention. I even like this twisted give-and-take we share.

"Change your clothes," I say. "Seriously. You're scaring the kids."

"One date," he persists. "Just one."

I shrug. I step away, gripping the straps of the chair, and turn around to catch up with Four and Pearl.

"That wasn't a no!" Jason calls out.

My back is turned to him, chair hiding me from view, and I'm glad for it because I can finally grin openly where he can't see me.

* * *

Jason is right, though. It's not a *no*.

* * *

True to his word, he doesn't give up.

I'm rocking out to the Pixies (a new obsession, thanks to Donovan) and working on my tan lines at the pool when an enormous shadow sucks the warmth out of the sky.

I open my eyes, pull down my headphones, and frown. "You're blocking everything."

Jason, the six-foot fuck-giant, looms overhead. He's at least wearing regular clothes this time—a loose T-shirt and joggers. He leans over and braces himself on my chair, his hands on my armrests. My eyes catch on the dark hair that runs up his forearms. I want to lick my lips, but I resist the urge.

"Alright, Trouble," he says, those sky-blue eyes locked on mine. "You and me need to have a conversation."

"About?" I ask innocently.

"What's it going to take to get you to go out with me?"

I tut. "Giving up already. Such a disappoint."

"No," he says. "Not giving up. Just giving you a chance to say *yes* before this gets ugly."

I snort on a laugh. "Give it your worst."

He straightens up. "Alright. You asked for it."

Then his eyes catch on Donovan and—*oh no.*

Donovan is at the lip of the pool, cleaning out the drain. He's got his back to us, and he doesn't see Jason approach.

"Jason, don't!" I tell him, but it's too late.

Jason grabs Donovan by the front of his shirt. He pulls him up so Donovan is on his feet and then shoves him outward. Donovan's heels are hanging off the lip of the pool, and he grabs Jason's wrist, his shoes struggling to regain traction. One shove, and Donovan will hit the water, uniform and all.

"Stop!" I shout.

Donovan twists and struggles, but Jason is strong, his grip tight, and he's not letting up. "Come out with me," Jason bargains, "and I'll let him go."

"Are you *twelve*?"

"Asshole," Donovan sputters as he struggles to get free.

We're not alone in this pool—there's at least three other boat owners here, plus the lifeguard. All adults. All pretending like they don't see what's going on.

No one does a damn thing. Not when it's Jason King.

No wonder he thinks he owns this island and everyone in it. *They let him get away with it.*

My teeth grind together.

"Okay!" I throw up my hands. "Whatever! Just…stop."

Jason finally pulls Donovan back from the edge of the pool and releases his grip.

Donovan's face is red. He scuttles quickly out of Jason's reach and says nothing.

I can practically see him retreating into his head.

He's embarrassed, defeated, and I hate Jason King for it.

It doesn't matter if he has the shoulders of a linebacker and the golden tan of a Greek god.

I *hate* Jason King.

"What time should I pick you up?" Jason asks casually. As though he didn't just have my best friend dangling over the edge of the pool.

I step over in front of him and slide my hands over his chest. His body is rock hard underneath the tight shirt. "Seven," I tell him. "Don't be late."

Then I go up on my tiptoes and lean in. He goes for the bait. Jason bends his tall frame, meeting me halfway, and his mouth nearly brushes mine—

When I shove him. As hard as I can.

Jason hits the water with a splash, clothes and all.

He might've won a date with me, but I don't have to be happy about it.

15

—

JASON

Mint chocolate chip.

That's Kenzi's favorite flavor.

I commit it to memory and pay for our waffle cones.

The local ice cream shop is peach pink with a walk-up window. There's an ornate sign out front with the word *Ahoy!* in bright letters, a ship painted behind the words, the exclamation point an upside-down ice cream cone.

It's a warm August night—not oppressive, but nice, the kind of heat that lingers like a good kiss.

Kenzi sits at one of the picnic benches outside of the shop. She's wearing overalls on top of a tight white shirt, which hugs her curves.

Her heart-shaped face is turned toward the sunset, ringlets of dark raven curls cascading down her shoulders.

She's a vision. I swing my leg over the bench, straddling it, and hand over her ice cream. "Your cone, m'lady."

"Merci."

"De rien."

She gives me a look like she's annoyed. Then she starts digging into her ice cream, giving me the cold shoulder.

"So are you going to pout all evening?" I ask her.

She shrugs. "I don't think we have anything to talk about. We have nothing in common."

"I bet we do. What's your favorite color?"

"Magenta."

"Mine, too."

She scoffs. "No, it isn't."

"Is this the face of a man who would lie to you?"

She rolls her eyes. But she seems a little softer around the edges. She cranes her neck to examine my cone. "What'd you get?"

"Half butterscotch, half rocky road."

"You're a professional."

"Don't you forget it." I hold it out for her. "Want a taste?"

"I don't have a spoon."

"I don't have cooties."

She gives in and runs her tongue over it, catching both flavors. A dollop of butterscotch gets on the tip of her nose, and I crook my finger and catch it.

She tilts away from me and rubs her nose over the back of her hand. "So is this your thing?" she asks.

"What do you mean?"

"I mean…you take a girl here, impress her with your obnoxious ice cream choices, dazzle her with the sunset, and then when she's feeling sugar-high and romantic, you get her to blow you in the dunes."

I scoff at that. "No way."

"No?"

"No. The dunes are too sandy."

She rolls her eyes. Enjoys her ice cream. I find myself studying the flick of her tongue.

"I'm just trying to get to know you," I tell her.

"Okay." She shifts, elbow on the table, fully facing me now. "Ask me something."

"What do you want to do?"

She cocks her head. "Professionally?"

"Like…with your life. What's important to you?"

"That is a question, isn't it?" She thinks, working over her ice cream. "I want to do something with music. Produce, maybe. Or write."

"You don't want to sing?"

She shakes her head. "No. It's the behind-the-scenes stuff that interests me."

"Can't take the limelight?" I ask.

She shrugs. "Not really."

"I've noticed that."

She squints at me skeptically. "What do you mean?"

"You hide," I tell her. "In books. Or you put those giant headphones on and hide in those. You're always…hiding."

She rolls her eyes. "Or maybe *you're* always soaking up the spotlight."

"Seems like we could learn something from each other, huh?"

That at least gets a small laugh from her. "Maybe."

She screws up her mouth, and her eyes flicker over me as though examining.

"What?" I finally ask, feeling like I'm under a microscope.

"It's just…strange. One-on-one? You're not so bad."

"Thanks. I think."

But she keeps staring, that inquisitive look in her eyes. Finally, she comes out with "Why do you bully Donovan so much?"

Of all the questions, I wasn't expecting that one. "We're just having fun," I tell her.

"Fun? Do you think Donovan thinks it's *fun*?"

I snort on a laugh. "C'mon. You two are hardly innocent, Trouble."

"It's different."

"Is it?" I challenge.

She frowns but doesn't say anything more on the subject.

KENZI

Jason walks me back home after we finish our ice creams. He leads me to the edge of the road and steps over the rope separating road from sand. He takes my hand to help me over the rope, and I let him. I take off my shoes, and he offers to carry them, so I let him do that, too. The sand feels warm between my toes, still sun-hot from the day. The long dune grass tickles my legs as we walk side by side through a hidden, narrow pathway.

The view is beautiful here.

Reds and purples streak across the sky and reflect across the sea. Even the white sand dunes look tinged with a soft, blushing pink.

His arm brushes against mine as we walk. His forearms have so much hair on them, and they tickle me.

There are parts of his body that seem so much like a man —the hair on his arms, his impressive height, the strength of his biceps.

But then he smiles—that mischievous, devil-may-care smile—and he looks so much like a boy.

We walk until the sky loses its color. When we get to the

end of the path, Jason puts my shoes on the ground and lets me balance with a hand on his shoulder as I step into them.

We leave the beach for the road and follow the elm trees and crickets to Four's house. The lights are on—kitchen, living room. I can see the flicker of the TV playing—probably one of Four's old western movies.

"How're you getting home?" I ask.

"I'll walk."

"I can get Four to drive you."

"Four?"

"Uh…Terry."

He grins. "I could use the walk. Thanks."

"Well." I lift a hand and invent some vague sweeping motion. "Thanks for the ice cream, I guess—"

Before I know it, his hand is on my face. We're close now, his perfect blue eyes trapped on mine. I can feel his breath, warm against my cheek.

"Can I kiss you?" he asks.

Yes, beg my lips, pouty and aching.

Yes, answers my heart, pounding against my rib cage.

Yes, scream my unrepentant, shameless teenage hormones.

But then I see Donovan in my mind's eye. My lust curdles.

I button my lips together and duck out of his embrace, pulling away. "Good night, Jason."

He opens his arms wide, imploring. "What's it going to take?"

I clutch my elbows and shrug.

He squints at me, like we're playing a game. "Give me a clue."

"Truth or dare?"

He raises his eyebrows. "Dare."

"I dare you to be less of a jackass to Donovan. See where that gets you."

With that, I slip inside the house, leaving Jason alone on the doorstep.

17

KENZI

*P*earl is already in her pajamas when I come home, but she still wants to know all the details. Where did we go? How did the date go? Was there a *kiss*?

I'm sitting in the kitchen and having second dessert—my nerves are wired, and I need it—and doing the best to field her questions when the house phone goes off. She picks it up, talks briefly, and then gives me a sly smile. She puts her hand over the receiver and says in a singsongy voice, "It's Jaaaay-*son.*"

I nearly choke on my cookie. Quickly, I scramble to my feet and dash upstairs. "I'll take it in my room!"

Cue me tripping over my own elephant feet to get into my bedroom, shutting the door, and quickly lifting the receiver. "Got it, Pearl! Thanks!"

"Keep it PG, darlings," Pearl says before she hangs up the phone, and I want to crawl under my bed.

"Hi," I say, forcing the word in a hard breath.

"Hey." I can practically hear Jason's cocky smile on the other end. "Your mom's hilarious."

I sit down on the edge of my bed. "How'd you get my number?"

"Well, technically, it's Terry's number. And he and my dad are friends. So."

"Oh." *Duh.* "What'd you want?"

"So that date didn't really go as planned."

I scoff. "What…so you're calling because you're mad I didn't kiss you?"

"No. That's not what I'm talking about. I didn't get to ask you all the questions I wanted to ask you."

"Like?"

He pauses, and then he asks, "Can we play a game?"

"Okay…"

"Truth or dare."

I snort a laugh. "Truth."

"Why do you feel like you have to hide?"

I pause. *Whoa.* That wasn't the question I expected him to ask. Maybe something like *does the carpet match the drapes* or *do you shave down there?* Not something…*real.*

I lean back against the huge, fluffy pillow against my headboard and deliberate my answer. "I guess…I've always felt like I'm getting in the way. Like I'm…"

"Trouble?"

"Yeah. Like that."

"Well, you *are* trouble," he tells me, his voice serious, "but you're not in the way. Hannsett Island is better with you in it."

Butterfly wings tickle my chest.

"Truth or dare, Jason?"

"Truth."

"Have you always had a hair trigger?"

"I guess sometimes I get a little…worked up."

"Go on…"

"It's like…I feel things. Really intensely. When I get angry, I see red and I can't back down."

I sigh dramatically. "I hate to be the one to tell you this, but…if you want to be a doctor someday, I'm pretty sure you're going to need to be able to keep a cool head in stressful situations."

"Yeah. You're not wrong about that."

"Have you tried yoga?"

"*Yoga?*"

"Yeah. It's like a sweat room full of MILFs doing downward dog. You'll love it."

He's chuckling again, at least. That's an improvement.

"Follow-up question," I add. "Is there anything that calms you down?"

He thinks about it. Really considering. "Water," he says.

"Water? Like…looking at water? Drinking water?"

"Swimming. I love swimming."

* * *

We go on like this all night:

"Truth," I say.

"What scares you?" Jason asks.

"Relying on other people. If I can't do something myself, I panic."

"Kenzi is not a team player. Got it."

* * *

"Truth," Jason says.

"Most embarrassing moment?" I ask.

"Easy. My swim meet last year. I had a stomach bug. I pushed through it anyway. Swam like a beast. Won first place."

"Wow, how embarrassing for you."

"It was, when the judge brought me my medal and I threw up on her. Like the exorcist. It was ugly."

* * *

"Truth," I say.

"What's your favorite memory?"

"Christmastime. I was eight. It was the first year me and Pearl were on our own. Her cooking is…questionable, at best. So we went out and got Chinese food."

Jason chuckles. "Is that a real thing people do?"

"In New York? Yeah."

"What'd you like about it?"

"I liked that it was just the two of us. We just…got to goof off together. We had a chopstick tickle fight. Stupid kid things."

"I love stupid kid things."

"Me too."

* * *

"Truth," Jason says.

"Is it easier for you to talk to me over the phone?" I ask.

"Yeah. I think so."

"Why?

"Sometimes, I feel like I've got to put on this face. I feel like people expect me to be a certain way. And then I just… become that."

"An asshole?"

"No, I mean…perfect. My dad is always like…*you're either a winner or a loser*. There's no in-between. And I get it, he expects big things from me, but…I don't know."

"It sounds like a lot of pressure."

"Yeah. Exactly. Right now, it's like…I'm just talking to air."

"Air that talks back."

"Something like that."

We lapse into silence, and for a minute, I just listen to him breath on the other end. I can feel the air between us, through the phone cords.

* * *

Through my curtains, the sky starts to glow orange.

"Pick dare," I tell him. "Truth or dare?"

"Dare," he obliges.

"I dare you to hang up."

There's a long silence on the other end and, for a moment, I think he did it.

"Jason?"

"…I dare *you* to hang up."

I can't help but grin.

18

DONOVAN

The water sucks.

So does sunshine.

Cloudless days. Salty air.

I judge all of it from *Healing Touch*'s stern.

The sun beats down on me. My uniform shirt is made with thick threads, and it's not long before I've got splotchy sweat stains on my pits and my back. I've got a jar of polish beside me and a washcloth in hand.

Polishing these monster boats is the worst task in the marina. It's pure manual labor. No way to speed up the process. Just hours of rubbing hard, clockwise circular motions into the fiberglass, and then repeating the same motion to clean the wax off.

A fucking pain in my ass.

The sound of a familiar voice makes me get to my feet. Across the dock, I see Kenzi on Terry's boat.

My heart lifts when I see her. Until I realize who she's talking to.

Jason King grips the mesh on her boat. They're chatting, leaning close. She's giggling.

Giggling.

Her eyes flick upward, and she spots me. She looks guilty suddenly. Like she's been caught with her hand in the cookie jar.

I try a wave. She gives me a small smile and waves back. Then she says something else to Jason before turning around and vanishing below deck.

So much for a happy reunion.

My chest is full of thorns when Jason climbs onto the *Healing Touch*. There's no way to avoid him—we're stuck on the same boat together now.

"Sup?" he says.

I don't answer. I just ask, "How was your date?"

"Good." Jason stops to think about it and then says, "Really good, actually."

My heart is hammering now, my blood charged.

"I guess you got what you wanted, huh?" I say.

Now, Jason shoots me a look. "It wasn't like that."

"Not like *what*?"

He contemplates his answer, then says, "We didn't have sex."

If *relief* were a scent, it would be salt-sweat, thick polish, and the words *we didn't have sex*.

Of course she wouldn't. Kenzi has standards. Principles. Kenzi is better than the likes of Jason King.

"Rejection is a bitch," I tell him and try not to sound quite so happy about it.

He's staring off into the distance, though, with a faraway look in his eyes. "She's different. I think we really made a connection."

I laugh. It's the worst sound I've ever made—a bitter bark of a noise. "You've got to be kidding me. The great Jason King. Felled by a pair of green eyes."

He shrugs. His nonresponse is almost worse than anything he could say.

I've *heard* him brag about his conquests. I've heard the

"locker room" talk.

But he's buttoning up about Kenzi. He's respecting her. It's almost like he's…

In love.

The thought makes my stomach lurch. This is worse than sex. This is something *real.* My teeth grind. "You've gone soft."

The edge of his mouth turns. I've hit a nerve. "Seems that way," he says, but his tone is thin. Irritated.

I can't help it. I provoke the lion. "Funny," I say. "I figured you're always hard. Or was that just for me?"

He launches at me, and immediately, I tense. I've avoided a lot of bloody noses and black eyes by knowing how to duck before a hit.

But the hit never lands.

I slowly reopen my eyes. Jason's hand is balled up into a fist, but it's locked by his side. He looks equally surprised.

Then he exhales. He unclenches his fingers to point at the deck.

"You missed a spot," he tells me. Then he climbs below deck and vanishes, leaving me there with my adrenaline still surging.

* * *

Cleaning the *Healing Touch* is a two-day job.

The next day, I'm bent over, sweat caking my shirt to my back, when I hear two pairs of feet clomp up the dock and come to a stop beside me.

"Hey. What's up?"

I glance up and feel my own sweat sting my eyes. Kenzi stands there, in her two-piece bathing suit and a pair of dark sunglasses.

She's smiling. My initial euphoria at seeing her is dampened by the fact that she's hanging out *with him.*

Jason hangs behind her, pool towel over his shoulder.

I frown. "What does it look like? My job."

"Washing the boat?"

"Polishing."

"Huh. We were on our way to the pool," Kenzi says—as though that's not obvious. "Want to take a break to get wet?"

"Can't." I don't want water. I want to be moody.

Jason leans forward and hangs off the mesh. "Can we help?"

19

———

KENZI

*I*t's especially hot.

The sun beats down on us. I have to tie my shirt in a knot, but I can still feel beads of sweat sliding down every part of my body.

Jason is working shirtless. I'm not complaining, except that it's distracting. He is insanely sculpted; I've never seen a body like his, except in the movies. Especially not on a *teenager*. It's hard for me not to stare—to follow the bead of sweat that drips down the center of his broad chest, over his toned stomach, and each pronounced ridge of his abdomen. When he buffs polish onto the boat, his biceps flex and those hard muscles roll down his back.

While shamelessly gawking, I feel a towel hit my face.

"Hey!"

Donovan just smirks from across the boat. "Distracted much?" he asks.

"N-no," I fumble. "Just thirsty."

"I can see that." Donovan doesn't stop looking smug.

Now Jason is looking at me, too, and my face feels hot and it's not from the sunburn. "Can you get me a bottle of water, babe?" I ask, making my voice sugar-sweet.

Aka please, please, please don't call my thirsty ass out in front of Jason.

Mercifully, Donovan gets to his feet. "You've got it, *hon.*"

I exhale as he leaves. He might tease hard, but he's not going to humiliate me in front of the boy that…well. I might have a *minor* crush on.

"Hey, can you grab me one, too, dude?" Jason calls out. "I'm sweating like a nun at church."

I laugh at that—obnoxiously loudly. Jason gives me a little confused grin. It was funny, but not *that* funny.

A small, itty-bity crush. I polish harder.

Suddenly, a string of curses comes from the stern. Donovan shouts and crashes around. Jason and I are immediately on our feet and rushing over.

"Dude, are you okay?" Jason asks.

"Fuck! It's huge!" Donovan is no longer on the deck—he's climbed up the railing of the boat, dangling half in and half out.

And then I see what he's talking about. A furry bundle bounces around the bottom of the boat. It looks like a beaver and is nearly as big, except instead of a beaver tail it has a thick ratlike tail.

A yelp leaves my lips before I can help it—I've seen New York subway rats, but nothing *that* big.

Jason, however, springs into action. He jumps into the center of the boat and stomps his feet loudly. "Other way, little dude!" he says. The giant rat-thing squeaks, its sharp nails clicking across the floor of the boat, and then finally finds the exit. It slides off the stern of the boat and flops into the water. It looks perfectly natural here and starts swimming quickly, zigzagging toward the tall grass.

My heart is hammering in my chest, and Donovan is still wrapped around the railing. Jason, however, breaks out into a laugh. He clasps Donovan on the shoulder hard.

"Bro, it's just a muskrat," he says. "Don't be a pansy."

Oh no. I know immediately that that's the wrong thing to say, because Donovan's ears go red. He swings his leg over, both feet on the boat now, and jerks away from Jason's touch. "I'm not your *bro*," he snaps, "so get your hand off me."

Uh-oh. Between the sun, the muskrat, and Donovan's short fuse, this is about to explode. I try to defuse it with "Maybe we should get back to—"

"I didn't mean anything by it, man," Jason says.

"Forget it," Donovan grumbles. He hops off the boat and onto the deck.

Jason looks at me blankly. "What'd I say?"

I sigh. "Donovan!" I climb over the railing and run down the deck after him.

20

DONOVAN

I'm aching.

My muscles ache. My heart aches. My soul aches. And I'm just tired. I'm so tired.

I make it down the deck, across the gravel, and head across the lawn toward my dad's trailer before I hear her calling after me.

"Donovan!" Kenzi cries out. "Wait up!"

My vision is blurring. I can't pretend to be okay anymore. I halt in my place, whip around, and face her. "You hate me," I state bluntly. "I get it. And now you've got a boyfriend and you'd rather spend time with him and *that's fine*—just stop rubbing it in my face."

Kenzi's panting lightly. She lifts her arms and then drops them. "Jesus Christ, I don't hate you, Donovan."

I blink and then blink harder, trying to clear the blurriness from my vision. "You don't?"

"No! I was afraid you'd hate me!" She waves her hand in my direction. "I mean, can you blame me?"

"I don't hate you. I could never." I pull my lips together. "Are you and Jason dating?"

"Would you stop being friends with me if we were?"

I don't even have to think about it. "No," I say. "I wouldn't."

She lets out a big sigh. Then she sits down on the grass and tosses her backpack in her lap. She opens it up and pulls something out.

"Here." She holds it out to me. It's a plain CD case. "You need variety in your scream-o."

"You made me a CD?"

"You're damn right I did."

"This is really cool. Thank you." I swallow hard. I don't want to give away the massive lump in my throat. "I'm sorry."

She bumps her shoulder against mine. "You should be. Because I'm a really good friend, and frankly, you're blowing it."

A relieved laugh escapes my lungs. I open the case. Kenzi's loopy handwriting scribbled in Sharpie on the CD, listing each track. I snort on a chuckle. "Fiona Apple?"

She drops her head against my shoulder. Her long hair tickles my neck. "Even a heartless bastard like you will love it," she says. "I promise."

* * *

She's right. I do love it. I put her CD on repeat and listen to it over and over until I fall asleep.

21

JASON

I don't get it.

One second, everything's fine. The next…

Donovan is acting like I shot his dog.

He won't look at me. Won't talk to me.

I'm good at a lot of things. I'm good at school. I'm good at swimming. I'm good at finishing a fight. I'm even good at cooking, believe it or not.

I'm *not* good at pretending things are okay when they're obviously not.

The next time I see them, Kenzi and Donovan are sitting together on the field that overlooks the marina. They've made themselves comfortable on one of the picnic benches, and it looks like they're enjoying lunch together.

When I get closer, I see they have a whole taco-building station set up. Little tin boxes filled with shells and toppings: cheese, shredded chicken, beans, sauces. They even have little plastic cups with jalapeño peppers and cilantro. You have to go off-island to get decent Mexican food, so I'm going to go ahead and guess this setup is the work of Kenzi's mom.

Kenzi and Donovan are sitting side by side. Donovan is

focused on picking apart his taco. Kenzi's eyes meet mine, but she quickly averts her gaze and looks away.

Okay. Enough is enough.

I walk over to their picnic table. When Kenzi sees me, her eyes get wide.

"Hey," I say. "What's up?"

Kenzi motions to her spread. "Taco Tuesday."

"I love tacos. Room for one more?"

"Uh...yeah," Kenzi says.

Donovan ignores me.

I sit, but I don't touch the food. "So, what? You're just going to give me the silent treatment? Because I called you a pansy?"

"That," Donovan says, "and a million other things." He looks at me, and those dark eyes of his are steely, like daggers. "If your posse was around, you wouldn't be talking to me. Or Kenzi."

I press my lips together. "What's it going to take for you to forgive me?"

Donovan lifts his eyebrows. "How long have you got?"

My eyes scan the table. I spot that little plastic cup of jalapeños—it's filled to the top. I put it on the table between us. "If I ate this whole thing. Right now. Can we be cool?"

He lifts his eyebrow dubiously, but his eyes don't leave mine.

"Um," Kenzi says. "That's like...a lot of jalapeños. I don't know if you should..."

Too late. My gaze locked on his, I put the cup to my lips and tilt it back in one go.

Kenzi's eyes go wide. So do Donovan's. "Holy shit..." he says.

"Not so bad," I say, crunching through the slices, the tiny seeds.

And then my mouth explodes.

I just make it to the trash can by the pool, where my body rejects the peppers and I hurl.

Dock Master Richard Donovan grabs me by the shoulder and drags me into his office, even though I tell him I'm fine.

And I am fine. I mean, my mouth is on fire, my throat feels like it's closing up, but Donovan and I are cool. I think.

I hope.

He gets me a milk carton from the kiddie supply, and I sip on it. It settles my stomach a little. When my throat is working again, I'm able to beg him: "Please don't call my dad. I'll do whatever you want. Just please, please don't call my dad."

I see where Donovan gets his stern gaze. He hands over the office phone. "He's already on the line."

I'd take the jalapeño sting over this lump in my throat any day.

I take the phone. "Hey."

"The harbor master said you were sick." My dad's voice is strong and steady. Controlled. "Is that true?"

"Uh…no. It's fine."

"Do you need me to come get you?"

He doesn't say it—I can hear the disappointment in his voice. *I knew you couldn't cut it. Disappointment. Loser. Pansy.*

"No, sir. I'm good."

"Are you sure?"

"Yeah."

"You're not giving them any trouble, are you? If you were…you know how that would look on us."

"No, sir. No trouble. Just something I ate. All good now."

A pause. The silence makes my stomach knot. Or maybe it's the spice. I hold it back either way.

"Should I be concerned?" he asks finally.

"Huh?"

"First, there was the incident with the boat. Then, I have to hear that you're running around in women's underwear. Now, this."

"It was a prank, Dad. We were just being idiots."

A labored sigh on the other end. "You're nineteen. Not a child. You act like that, people are going to think you are a—"

And then he says a word I've heard him say a thousand times before. It still feels like knives in my chest every time he says it, though.

"Yes, sir," I respond, the phrase automatic. "I understand."

"You understand that everything you do reflects on our family."

"Yes, sir."

"Good." There's a pause. "Come home tonight. Your mother wants you home for dinner more than once an eon."

Then the call ends. But my nerves won't untangle.

I hand the phone back to Donovan's dad. "Thanks."

"Feel better," he says in a growl, which sounds more like *get out of my office.*

My throat thickens, and I feel myself wanting to get sick again, but I swallow it back. He walks me down the dock and back to the *Healing Touch*. Makes sure I have everything I need. I get inside and count to five until I can't hear his footsteps on the planks anymore. Then I dive to the bathroom and puke until nothing else will come up.

* * *

I sleep it off for a couple of hours. I'm still feeling a little clammy that evening, but I leave the shelter of the boat and head up the docks.

There's a family a couple of boats down. A kid, maybe six, is sitting with his dad, who's teaching him how to fish. The kid looks fascinated as his dad globs a mess of bait on the end of the hook. It makes me grin. And feel sad for some reason I can't place.

Kenzi and Donovan are still hard at work. They're buffing and polishing one of the yachts at the far end of the marina. Kenzi is bent over. Not for the first time, I notice how nice her ass looks. The curving arch of her foot when she stands on her toes. That small dip where her shoulder meets her neck. I love that spot on women—I love kissing it. She's got her hair pulled back today, and as though she feels me staring, she rubs the sweat from her neck, right *there.*

Which is when she turns, and I smile. Kenzi lights up.

"Man of the hour!" Kenzi calls out.

My heart swells, but I try to play it cool. "Sup?"

"Grab a sponge, Hotshot," Donovan says.

There's an extra sponge and bucket on the dock, so I grab both and climb over the railing to join them.

Kenzi hops over to me and glances around furtively before she pulls something out of the bikini bra of her swim-suit. "We made you something," she whispers.

It's a piece of paper. I unfold it. When I do, there's no more playing it cool—I can't help the dumb grin I feel spreading across my face.

It's a drawing of me (and a pretty damn good drawing, too) with flames coming out of my mouth like a dragon. I've got a star attached to my chest like a sheriff, only it says "#1 Hotshot" with a hot pepper drawn on the badge.

"Aw. Thanks, guys. I look like a superhero."

"We're like the Three Musketeers!" Kenzi says.

"The Three Muskets," I chime in.

"No," Donovan says, "The Three Muskrats."

We burst out laughing at that.

22

KENZI

*H*annsett Island isn't big. You can get around it entirely by bike or—if you're Jason King—by golf cart. Beyond the marina, there's the main town which is comprised of one long street. On it—a grocer, a bookstore, an ice cream shop, and a handful of boutique clothing stores, not to mention the required shop for swimwear and pool toys.

Four lives on the north side of the island, where there are resort houses and summer rentals that are identical save the bright colors. Pelican pink, sunflower yellow, lime green.

With the summer winding to a close and no movement from the waitlist on Berklee College, Pearl has decided I need to come up with a "backup plan." She also figured out that the only way to get me to accomplish said backup plan is to trap me in the house and inform me that I can't go to the marina until I've figured something out.

Which is how I end up on house arrest in August, staring moodily at the desktop computer Four let me cart into my bedroom. So far, my options are limited:

On Craigslist, there's an ad for an assistant at a record

store. The ad specifically requests a female, 18-25, *picture required with submission of resume.*

Double ugh.

I keep clicking. There's an internship for a PR assistant for a musical group in England, but what are my chances of getting *that*?

I'm calculating how much of my soul to sell to get Pearl off my back when I hear, "Kenzi!"

It's strange. It's Jason's voice, but it sounds nearby. I open my bedroom door, but I don't see anyone.

"Kenzi! Over here!"

I turn around and yelp when I see him. My room is on the second floor, and Jason is *in the window.* He's grinning like an idiot, perched on the tree branch like a goddamn monkey.

I open my window, a smile I can't help plastered on my face. "What the hell are you doing?"

"Busting you out, obviously."

"Is Donovan here?"

Jason points down. Donovan stands at the bottom of the tree, his hands in his pockets.

"I don't have a death wish," Donovan says.

God, my boys are a sight for sore eyes.

"Alright," I say, "scoot over."

Jason reaches out and takes my hand. Carefully, I climb out the window and follow him onto the tree branch. Jason's strong arm winds around me, and I don't worry about falling, not when I'm in his grip. We shimmy from branch to branch, and Donovan reaches up to help us down one by one.

"Nice getaway car," I say as I hop off the tree, brushing myself off.

The golf cart sits on Four's back lawn.

"We work with what we've got," Donovan says. He then climbs into the driver's seat.

"Wait, *Donovan* is driving?" I ask as I climb in the back.

Jason piles in beside me, his long limbs squished in the tight space.

"I had the same thought," Jason says. "I felt safer in the tree."

"I can drive just fine," Donovan says, and the car lurches forward unconvincingly. I grip the side to stay in place.

"Where are we going?"

"Where *aren't* we going?" Jason answers mysteriously. He has a cat that swallowed the canary smile—like he has some big Mona Lisa secret he can't wait to share with us.

I'll admit it: my crush on Jason has only gotten worse the more we hang out. How couldn't I? He's a beautiful boy, with linebacker shoulders, a disarming smile, and he's taller than most of the adults I know. His dark hair blows in the wind as we start down the road, and I itch to run my fingers through it and mess it up.

His arm brushes against mine as we bounce down the road, those fine hairs tickling, and it makes me shiver. Donovan glances behind him, and I must have drool on the corner of my mouth because he rolls his eyes at me.

Donovan is beautiful in a different way—a quiet, brooding boy with sharp features and intense dark eyes.

It's strange to me that I found myself attached to these two boys all summer. Stranger still that, once September rolls around, I'm going to go back home to Queens and I won't get to see them every second of every day anymore.

"We're here," Donovan announces as he pulls the golf cart off the road and into a parking lot behind a giant warehouse.

I ask. "And *here* is...?"

"Boat graveyard," Jason replies.

We get out and follow Donovan around the side of the building. Sure enough, on the other side, it's a boatyard.

If you've never seen a boat out of water, it's a bizarre sight. Like a giant whale on display. There's a huge metal frame on wheels at the edge of the water with a long double sling in it, which, I imagine, is how they scoop the boats onto dry land.

Donovan winds us through the yard with purpose and then comes to stop in front of one. "Check this one out," he says.

The sailboat in question is hoisted up on these metal stands that do *not* look like it should be able to hold it up. The keel—which is boat-term for *the big fin at the bottom of the boat*, I've learned—makes it look twice as big. The sail is wrapped up in a shabby cloth, and the boat itself looks pretty beat-up. There are more than a couple of dents in it, holes in the sides, and damage to the windows.

It's no surprise that it's out of the water, getting repairs.

Sorry, *she*. Donovan corrected me about that once. *All boats are shes.*

"What happened to it?" I ask. I feel oddly sorry for the thing. It's like witnessing a dog tied to a pole with a too-small collar. Neglect looks ugly, even if the item in question has no feelings.

Still. I may never be a skipper, but this summer has certainly taught me one thing: boats have souls. Even damaged ones like this.

Especially the damaged ones, if you ask me.

"It's abandoned," Donovan responds. "Come on."

Then he grabs the ladder, which is at least a solid three feet off the ground, and hoists himself up.

"Wait…we're going *inside?* This feels a little like breaking and entering."

"You won't get in trouble," he reassures me. "I promise."

I frown at the thin metal stand keeping the boat propped up. Logically, I know I'm not going to topple over a thirty-foot sailboat. But the nagging parts of my anxiety are dubious.

Jason helps me up the ladder, and Donovan helps me into the boat. But when I climb onto the landing, my Converse slip on the damp boards. Jason catches my arm, saving me from a tumble off the side of the boat and onto the gravel below. For a second, my body brushes against his, and I feel his hard-muscled chest underneath the thin layer of cotton.

"Careful, Trouble." He grins at me.

"Thanks," I reply, hating how breathless and girly my voice sounds.

We climb aboard, and Donovan pushes open the latch so we can go below deck. It's dim inside, and I can only make out shadows and shapes.

"There's no electricity," Donovan explains, "but we've got this."

He lights a match and, seconds later, ignites a brass gas lantern that hangs from the ceiling. Now, I can see the ship in all of its glory.

It's old—that's obvious. The walls are lined with wood, and there are patches where the wood has been punched out. It's been mostly emptied out, nothing on the shelves but a couple of books. There are a couple of old-school touches—the gas lantern, navigation table with an old water-stained map on it, and some kind of compass that looks like it came from a different era. In short, everything that appeals to my anachronist heart. The upholstery looks newer than the rest of it, though, dark cushions that line the benches.

"Whose boat is this?" Jason asks.

Donovan sits down, and with a flick of his wrist, the match goes out. "Mine."

"What?"

"It was abandoned on one of the mooring balls. The original owner was a patient at the medical center who took a turn for the worst. The family didn't want it, so they handed it over to my dad. Dad said if I can patch up the holes and get it back into shape, I can have it."

"So you're going to…what. Sail the coast?"

"Maybe."

"What about college?" Jason asks.

Donovan shrugs. "Scholarship money didn't come through. So. I'll just have to try next year."

"Oh, shit. I'm sorry, man."

"It is what it is."

An uncomfortable silence washes over us. It's easy to forget that we all come from different worlds. I can take a year off knowing full well that, when I'm ready, Pearl and one of her husbands will take care of all my expenses. Jason doesn't have to think twice about admission—he's guaranteed a spot.

Donovan isn't afforded the same luxuries. It's a sharp reminder.

"You need a first mate?" I ask, steering the topic away.

There's a hint of amusement in Donovan's eyes at that. "Yeah, maybe. You want to spend your gap year here?"

"Seriously?"

"Seriously."

"I'll think about it," I say. But my grin stretches too wide across my face and gives me away. I can't think of *anything* better than spending the winter with Donovan—no parents, no rules. Just the water and us, doing whatever the hell we want to do.

"What are you going to call her?" Jason asks.

"What do you mean?"

"The boat? She needs a name."

"I haven't thought about it."

I gasp. "That's *all* I would think about! Okay. Emergency brainstorm time."

Donovan suggests the *TARDIS*, *Muskrat King*, and *Fuck You I Own A Boat*.

Jason suggests, *Nightrider*, *Skipper Syndrome*, and *Captain Emo*.

I give my suggestion, but Donovan furrows his brow. "*Deck Boy*?" he repeats.

"No, Dock *Buoy*. B-U-O-Y. It's a pun."

They both think about it for a second too long before they burst into laughter. "Yeah," Jason says. "That's definitely the winner."

"So what do you do for fun on a boat with no electricity?" I ask.

Donovan opens up the navigation table and pulls out a deck of cards, tossing it onto the table. "Name the game."

"Poker," I say.

"I heard *strip poker*," Jason counters as he starts to shuffle. "Who else did?"

"I'm game." I grin.

"Deal us in," Donovan says, completing our circle.

* * *

As it turns out, Donovan and I *suck* at poker.

Jason and I have a spark, but Donovan and I share a soul —we have a whole language of eyebrow twitches, squints, and slightly upturned lips. I can read him like a book, and he can read me. Which makes neither of us very good at bluffing each other.

Donovan and I both get down to our underwear. When I have to take off my bra, Donovan gives me a blanket to cover myself with—which Jason says is cheating—but that's too bad. Meanwhile, Jason has only lost a pair of socks.

Donovan folds and I, finally, manage to get one over on Jason. "Read it and weep," I tell him, putting down three of a kind.

"Alright, Trouble, you've got me." He reaches behind and yanks his shirt over his head, tossing it to the side.

And just—ouch. He's so hot it's physically painful. He's got that broad linebacker's chest, sculpted and strong. I squeeze my thighs a little tighter to relieve the pulsing pressure and turn my attention to shuffling cards instead.

"Uh—yep. That'll do."

Donovan gives me a look. He doesn't have to say anything —we speak without words, and right now, he's saying, *You're shameless, Kenzi.*

Yeah, yeah. I know. But I'm eighteen and a virgin, and this is as close as a soft-bellied, splotchy-faced girl like me is going to get to the sun, so he can put up with it for a night.

We go another round, but this time, my luck has turned. I grumble as I turn over my cards—a high seven—and Donovan bursts into laughter.

"Your tell is *so bad*!" he says.

I scoff. "What tell?"

"You touch your earlobe," he says and then does it, rubbing his ear between his thumb and finger. "Every time you lie."

"*Ugh.* You two suck." Which is about when I realize I'm out of clothes to take off. All I have are my panties.

"You don't have to take them off," Donovan says, reading my mind. I hear the concern in his voice—he doesn't want me to feel pressured to strip in front of them.

And this is one of those decisions, right?

Go the safe route. The predictable route. End the game, go home to Pearl and Four, and eventually leave Hannsett Island completely. Maybe forever, if Pearl and Four get divorced before summer comes back around, which is a high probability.

And even if they don't? Jason is going to college. Donovan and his ship are going who knows where. I may never see them again.

I make a decision. I shrug, playing it cool. "Rules are rules."

Then I remove the blanket, stand from the bench, and move my hands to the band of my panties.

"Wait," Jason says. Then he crocks his finger. "Come here. A woman should never have to take off her own panties."

I'm surprised by my own brazenness as I stride forward and stand in front of him. Jason looks up at me, and…something shifts in those blue eyes. He looks like he wants to devour me. His hands slip up my legs, and he hooks two fingers underneath the sides of my panties. He doesn't pull them down right away, though—instead, with his eyes still locked on mine, he gently kisses my thigh.

"Is this okay?" he asks.

My throat is so dry with want, I almost don't have the ability to conjure up words. Then an idea possesses me. I rake my fingers through his soft black hair.

"Truth or dare?" I ask.

He smiles. "Dare."

"I dare you to take them off…without ever looking away from my eyes."

His eyes sharpen at the challenge. "Can do."

Jason slowly rolls my panties down my legs. I should feel shy, but I don't.

I feel like—maybe for the first time—I'm completely in control.

Especially because those brilliant blue eyes don't leave mine, not for a second. Not even when I'm completely naked in front of him.

"Truth or dare, Trouble?" he asks me.

"Truth."

"How badly do you want to kiss me right now?"

Now my cheeks get hot. *This* is what being exposed feels like. "Um…badly."

He doesn't let me off the hook. "Go on."

"Like I'll die without it—"

I barely finish before Jason grabs the backs of my thighs and pulls me down with him. I gasp, now straddling his lap. The tip of his nose brushes my cheek. His breath feels quick and hot on my face.

"Truth or dare?" I whisper.

"Dare."

I push my lips against his. He makes a small surprised noise against my mouth, but then I feel his tongue probing, opening me. Tasting me.

Am I doing this right? I'm not sure and I venture into his mouth curiously. His hands slide up my thighs, holding me tightly against him. I can feel the hardness of his denim jeans. The heat of his kiss. He sighs into my mouth and I think —*yes*. I'm doing *something* right.

"Well," Donovan's voice filters through. "That's my cue."

He stands, grabs his clothes, and tosses his shirt back on. But then Jason surprises us both. He grabs Donovan's wrist before he can leave, holding him in place, and says, "Or you can stay."

Donovan glances over at me, his dark eyes inquisitive.

I agree with, "Stay. Please?"

Donovan worries his bottom lip between his teeth. "Alright," he finally says and then sits back down. His pants are still lumped in a pile in his hands, and he puts them aside on the table.

Jason nods to where Donovan is sitting. "Why don't you go lie down beside him?"

I do. I stretch out on my back on the cushioned bench, my head on Donovan's thigh. He draws his fingers through my hair instinctively, and I reach for his arm. I pull his hand in close and kiss that leather bracelet he always wears, and then I kiss his palm. His eyes meet mine, and they're full of affection.

Jason stands over me. He sheds his clothes. I can see the excitement in his electric blues, the hunger. It makes my blood hot. "Have you done this before?" he asks.

"What," I reply. "Have I been torn up by two dudes at once?"

I'm nervous as hell, and my sense of humor is dark and strange.

"I mean…are you a virgin?"

"Uh…yeah. Is that okay?"

"If it's good by you, it's good by me."

"Hey." Donovan gets my attention now. He cups my face, tilts my chin look at him. He's always had the most intense, striking dark eyes, and now I find myself swallowed up in them. Tenderly, his thumb strokes my cheek. "If you want this to stop," he says—and he's using his best friend voice now, "at any point. Just say the word. Okay?"

I nod. "I know." I reach out and cup the back of his neck, petting his hair—I *adore* this man. And I know it's weird—I know this is insane and not at all how I pictured it would go—but I'm suddenly so grateful to have my best friend here for my first time. He'll protect me. No matter what. I feel utterly safe and warm with him here.

Jason climbs on top of me and—God. His body is beautiful. The light from the lantern casts a sheen of gold over his taut muscles.

I touch his jaw and draw him in, kissing him deeply. I've decided I love the way Jason kisses me. There's nothing uncertain about it—he swoops his tongue in my mouth, tasting me deeply, boldly. He devours me completely, and I succumb to him.

When Jason enters me, there's a pinch, and I whimper. I must shed a tear or two because Donovan strokes my cheek, runs his fingers through my hair, and asks me if I'm okay.

"I'm okay," I'm murmur, "keep going. Please."

Jason is gentle, slow, deliberate. The burst of pain fizzles into something bearable, and then something enjoyable, and then something *so goddamn good* I have to bite my bottom lip to keep myself from screaming.

Jason is the ocean. He rolls over me in waves, swooping, crashing.

Donovan is the moon. He pulls me, guides me, orbits me.

The three of us together are lips and tongues and

squeezed fingers and heat. The air is dense with the smell of old wood—like the bottom of a cork in a wine bottle—and the musk of our own sweat and arousal.

Jason's lips tickle my throat as he moves over me. He tells me that I'm beautiful. He tells me that I'm *so fucking beautiful*. I feel a heat rise through me, making me blush.

"You're right there, aren't you?" Jason murmurs in my ear.

I gasp and nod. My throat gets tight, and I feel my toes curl. My body is shaking, thighs trembling, everything in me as taut as piano wire. Everything in me is screaming for a release, but I'm clinging to the edge.

"Then let go."

"I'm afraid," I whisper.

"Of what?"

"I'm afraid I'll shatter apart."

"I'm here," Donovan says, his voice low and strong, anchoring me to solid ground. His fingers trail through my hair, nails tickling my scalp. "I'm right here."

On instinct, I reach out and find Donovan's hand.

DONOVAN

I take Kenzi's hand in mine. Her fingers curl and tighten.

"Donovan!" she moans.

And it shouldn't get to me, but—

Jason was wrong. That night on the beach, he told me he would fuck her this summer. He told me she would cum screaming his name.

And he was *wrong.* She came with my name on her tongue. Not his.

I squeeze her hand back.

"That's good," I whisper to her, encouraging, "You're doing really good…"

KENZI

When I come down, I'm floating.

I feel soaked in sweat. I'm wet, sticky. I don't feel at all like a solid form. I am my racing heartbeat. My shuddery breath.

Jason pulls out of me once he finishes, and I feel empty. It's strange—thirty minutes before, this was all I knew. Now, without Jason inside of me, I feel like something is missing.

He kisses my chest, my neck, and then my lips. "Are you okay?" he asks.

A laugh bubbles up and escapes me. "Amazing," I say. "That was...amazing."

I realize I'm still gripping Donovan's hand. I pull it to my lips and give the back of his fingers a kiss, too.

"Thank you," I say. "Both of you."

Donovan shifts in his seat slightly, trying to adjust. But in only his briefs and a shirt, it's hard not to see the swell of him.

I sink into the cushion, becoming one with the material. Meanwhile, Jason stands up.

"Hey, dude, I've got you," Jason says. He comes over and pats Donovan's chest.

"What—?" Donovan starts.

Jason reaches into Donovan's briefs, pops out his erection, and drops to his knees.

"Holy...fuck..." Donovan sputters, which is what everyone is thinking.

Because now Jason King has Donovan down his throat. His fingers clench on Donovan's shirt, and his head bobs low. Steady, determined swoops in Donovan's lap.

I can't help tearing my eyes away. My lips go dry, and I wet them with the tip of my tongue. Donovan's eyes roll back. His moan is low and long.

I don't release Donovan's fingers, and neither does he. He's quiet, for the most part, save a couple of shuddered breaths and small, swallowed swears. He looks concentrated, his eyebrows knit. I can tell when he finishes because his fingers squeeze mine again, tightly, and then his grip slackens.

Jason rises and wipes his mouth with the back of his hand. He dips down to meet Donovan's lips, and they almost-kiss. It's a soft, tentative thing, a brush of lips, and there's something very...*sweet* about it. Then Jason scoops up the blanket from the bench, cocoons it around himself, and then says, "You need to get this place a proper bed."

"Couldn't agree more," says Donovan, his breath light.

Jason tosses the blanket out on the floor and settles down on that instead. It's the only place where there's enough room for the three of us. I climb over to lie beside him, and Donovan follows suit, trapping me in the middle.

For a while, we just breathe together. It's not an uncomfortable silence. It's just...*silence*. All three of us taking in what just happened. Letting this insane night settle into our bones.

Insane. And *amazing*. Here, between the two of them, I feel like I'm exactly where I need to be. For the first time, I'm not a burden. I'm not in the way. I'm *right* where I'm supposed to be, and it feels good.

I curl up against Donovan's chest and tug Jason's arm around me, savoring their body heat.

"Hey, so..." Jason starts, a small strain in his voice, his breath brushing my hair, "are you guys...uh...going to tell anyone about this?"

Donovan and I make eye contact—and make a silent agreement.

"We're the Three Muskrats," I say and lace my fingers through Jason's, pulling him tighter. "What happens on the boat, stays on the boat."

KENZI

*W*e make an unlikely trio…

Donovan, the outcast, the quiet queer boy whose humor is as dark as his clothes.

Jason, prom king, pretty boy, the popular boy with a secret heart of gold.

And me. The weird music nerd, who always has a notebook and pair of headphones within arm's reach.

But it works. Somehow.

We spend August attached at the hip. We play truth or dare. We go to the beach, the pool, or sometimes just hang out in the woods by Donovan's trailer. We have our own unwritten rules. For example, when Jason's friends are over, Donovan and I know to give Jason a wide berth. He still, after all, has the *popular boy* role to play. But he barks at them anytime someone teases Donovan, and eventually, he stops inviting them over completely. Jason and I spend a lot of the day helping Donovan with his various tasks around the marina. It's grueling work, but with the three of us, it gets done quickly, which gives us more time to hang out with him afterward.

We find ways to share each other. During the day, I pull

Jason into the laundry room, climb him like a tree, and kiss him until we're both swollen-lipped and breathless. Donovan and I set aside time every week for the new *Dr. Who* episodes (he's obsessed, and now I'm sucked into it, too). Jason joins us but doesn't have the patience for TV, so he mostly runs back and forth making popcorn or getting snacks. Sometimes, I catch him press a small kiss to the back of Donovan's neck, which makes the other boy shiver.

As for Donovan and me—we're closer than ever. I lay my head in his lap. He pets my hair. Sometimes, I slip my fingers in his and just savor the warmth of his palm, the strength of his grip.

Sometimes, it's just a *look* or a *smile*. A knowing that only we share. I treasure our secret, stolen little intimacies.

No one—not even Pearl—would understand this. But they don't have to. It's ours and ours alone, and I like it that way.

I find myself craving the time I get to spend in the marina with my boys. The worst part of each day is when Pearl starts calling my name from the parking lot and I have to hop in the car to head back to Four's summer house.

I'm always bone-tired by the end of the day, though. And my feet are always sore.

I inherited my dad's feet—flat, wide duck feet.

During the school year, I squeeze them into too-narrow flats, so when I come home, they always feel tender and ache.

Donovan, Jason, and I run around barefoot like savages. I burn the soles of my feet on the sun-hot boards of the dock. I stroll across the gravel walkways and run around the bare ground by Donovan's trailer, which is littered with sticks and acorns.

When I shower, I feel the bottoms of my feet. They're smooth like sea glass, but the skin has toughened. It makes me feel strong. Viking-like.

Maybe I, too, am getting stronger.

* * *

But my feet aren't the only thing about me that's different.

Because a couple weeks later, I miss my period.

I tell myself I'm paranoid. I'm being dramatic. It's a whole lot of *nothing*.

But three pregnancy tests all tell me the same thing.

I'm fucked.

KENZI

Everything is changing.

The leaves are turning color, from green to orange and red. The weather is crisper. September has bite.

We'll be leaving Hannsett Island soon. Back to my mom's apartment in Queens, where the air tastes like cigarette smoke and car exhaust instead of sea salt.

Paradise couldn't last forever, anyway.

Donovan and Jason want to hang out as much as possible in the remaining time we have, but I keep making excuses to avoid them. I tell them it's my time of the month (I wish). I tell them I'm not feeling well. I tell them Four is making us engage in a little "family time."

So when Pearl and Four take me back to the marina to get some boat time in while the weather is still nice, I've run out of excuses.

We board *Sweet Serenity,* and Four and Pearl go below deck. I linger up top.

It's starting to get chilly here. A lot of the boats have awnings over them. They're locked down and closed up. The swans have left their nests. The pool is empty, shut down.

For the first time, I realize that I'm going to miss this place when summer is over.

I don't see Donovan or his dad anywhere. There's activity on the *Healing Touch*, though. Jason's dad is sitting on the deck. He's wearing a wool sweater stretched across his broad chest. His mouth is pulled into a focused frown underneath his graying beard. He's opened up a storage hatch, and he's pulling things out, making small piles.

I climb over the railing and hop onto the deck. I cross so I'm standing in front of his boat.

"Hi, Mr. King," I say.

He glances up at me and offers a smile. "Kenzi. How's your mother?"

"Good." I rock back and forth on my bare feet, feeling small and awkward. "Is Jason here?"

He shakes his head and turns his attention back to his project. "No. He's back at the house."

"Oh." A thought strikes me. Maybe not the best thought. Or the worst. But I'm out of options. And Jason's dad *did* tell me over dinner to come to him if anything…came up.

"What're you doing?" I ask.

"Putting the boat away for the summer. All good things must come to an end."

"Cool." I bite my lip. "Can I get your advice about something?"

"Sure."

"It's…kind of personal."

He looks up at me. Those steel blues—they're all Jason's eyes. But these crinkle with concern. "Come aboard," he tells me, so I do.

* * *

I don't know how I muster up the courage, but I tell him.

It comes out in a burst. All the words that I've kept pent up inside of me.

I tell him that I had sex with his son—I leave the details and the Donovan out of it. I tell him about missing my period, and the pregnancy tests, and the results that came after.

Mr. King is silent. He listens to me the whole time, letting me get it out.

We're sitting in the navigation room. It's a small area with a circular table between us. I have a glass of water in front of me, but I haven't touched it. I haven't stopped talking since I sat down.

Surrounded by all this dark oak, I feel like I'm in a confessional. Maybe that's why I find it so easy to spill my guts to him.

When I finally go quiet, he lets the silence hang between us for a minute. He doesn't look angry or confused. He just looks contemplative, his fingers tented at his mouth. Finally, he lowers them and asks, "Does your mother know?"

I shake my head. "No, but I plan on telling her, I just... haven't found the right moment."

"That's good," he interrupts. "Keep it that way. She never has to know. And neither does Jason."

I blink. I'm not sure what kind of advice I was expecting, but *hide your pregnancy from your mother* wasn't at the top of the list. "Okay..."

"It will ruin her life. And his. Do you understand that?"

A knot forms in my throat. "I guess..."

"Do you have to?"

"What do you mean?"

"Do you have to guess? Your mother has a unique method of survival by attaching herself to affluent men. I imagine that would get much harder were she to have a pregnant teenager."

The knot in my throat is now the size of Jupiter, and growing.

"And then there's my son," he says, and his voice—already deep, already dark—drops about ten degrees. "Jason is on the track for an extraordinary medical career. He graduated with honors. He's the top of the swim team. And he's attending John Hopkins in the fall. Having a child right now would obliterate his future."

I can't speak. The knot is too tight.

But then he softens. He reaches across the table and grips my shoulder and squeezes gently. "You did a good thing telling me, Kenzi. I'll set you up for an appointment at the medical center tomorrow. We'll get this taken care of."

"Taken…care of?" I echo the words like I'm learning the English language.

"It's better this way." He stands then. "Come here."

I follow his lead. He takes me in his arms and hugs me like he's my father. He smells smoky, like bergamot, with the hint of something sweet, like apple. His heavy cologne makes my stomach twist.

"It's going to be okay," he tells me, and he sounds so certain of it that, in that moment, I almost believe him.

* * *

Four lets me borrow his bike.

He's thrilled, I think. Look at me, getting exercise. Fresh air. All-American fun.

Impossible to tell him that the reason I need the bike is because I don't want anyone to know where I'm going.

Mr. King set me up with an appointment. 1:00 p.m. at the Lighthouse Medical. To get things "taken care of." Don't be late.

I strap my headphones around my ears, tuck my Walkman into my backpack, and blast music as I bike up the road. I let the music clear out my thoughts. It's like my ears are open windows and the music is a hefty cross-breeze, blowing away anything in its path.

Because when I let myself think, my thoughts are chicken wire. It hurts to cross them.

You're doing the right thing, he'd said. *You're making the right choice.*

Maybe he's right, you know? He's the adult here. I'm a dumb girl who got herself stuck in a dumb spider's web of problems I can't easily wiggle out of this time.

As I get closer, the lighthouse peeks out first from the horizon. And then the hospital itself. It strikes me how big it is. How impressive.

How small I feel standing next to it, straddling my bike.

I need to go inside. But I can't. My feet are stuck to the ground.

I can't do this, I think. The thought is a lump in my throat, a weight on my chest.

I can't do this.

"Kenzi?"

Donovan is standing there. The sight of him is both a surprise and a relief, and I nearly fall off my bike. I adjust, keeping balance, and ask, "What're you doing here?"

He's by the bike rack, pulling his own bike out. It's worn and the pedals click loudly when he walks it beside me. "Last day of my summer program."

"How'd it go?"

He makes a gagging sound. I laugh. Too loudly.

He knits his eyebrows. "What are *you* doing here?"

Um…

"Here to celebrate you, obviously. Happy graduation."

That pulls a smile from him. "Seriously?"

"Seriously. We can do whatever you want."

He glances over his shoulder. "We should wait for Jason."

"No," I say too quickly. The thought of seeing him right

now sends my heart pounding. "I mean…I thought this could just be the two of us. For old time's sake."

He bites his lower lip briefly in thought. Then he swings his leg over his bike and says, "C'mon."

We speed down the road, away from the medical center, even as I feel the pull of anxiety tightening like a noose around my neck with every pedal push.

* * *

We end up at the very top of the clay cliffs. We find a spot where the grass is cut shorter and flop down, head to head, watching the clouds. It's chilly up here, but the sun is hot, and it warms my skin.

"What's the deal with Jason's dad?" I ask after a while.

Donovan glances over at me, his eyebrows knit. "What do you mean?"

"I mean…what do you know about him?"

Donovan thinks about it, then says, "My family has a… weird relationship with the Kings."

"How so?"

A sigh escapes him. "We didn't always live in a trailer. We had a house in Syracuse. Dad was an accountant. Mom was a teacher. We were comfortable. And then Mom got cancer. He really loved her, so…my dad went all out. The best doctors. The best hospital. That's how we came here. I was thirteen. It was supposed to be temporary. But…she never got better. She fought it. Hard. For two years. But…well…"

His voice trails. I reach up and touch his hair, running my fingers through it. "I'm sorry."

"Me too. Anyway. In case you haven't noticed, this place… isn't cheap. My dad had to sell the house. It ate up his savings. Everything we had, basically. Mr. King…took pity on us, I guess. He gave my dad a job at the marina as a way to settle his debts. And we've been working it off ever since."

"So he got you out of debt? That's generous."

Donovan bites his lip. "Sort of."

"What's the *sort of* part?"

"Well...it makes you think. What does the guy value more than money? *Control.* My dad can't make a move without Mr. King's say-so. He's in his pocket. For good. Which is fine, as long as you stay on Mr. King's good side."

"And if you don't?"

Donovan lapses into a long, dark pause. "I don't even want to think about the ways he could make me and my dad's lives a living hell."

And this coming from *Donovan*, the guy who is bullied on a regular basis.

A knot twists in my stomach and won't come undone.

He glances back at me, those chestnut browns meeting my gaze. "Why do you ask?"

"No reason." I purse my lips together and turn my head away from Donovan, staring off into the wide ocean below. A seagull swoops across the distance, and I feel instant envy.

* * *

Applications will be the death of me. I have a fire lit under my ass now, though. At least applying to internships keeps my mind off my little (big) problem.

"Kenzi!" Pearl calls from downstairs. "The phone for you!"

I pick up the landline in my room. "Hello?"

"Kenzi." The voice on the other side sends my nerves on edge. Mr. King continues. "I heard you missed your appointment."

I swallow. Hard. But better to be honest, right? "Yeah...I think I just need time. To think about it."

"I see." A lengthy pause. "Would a check help?"

"Sorry?"

"Money. I can help with your college fund, perhaps."

"Oh, I'm not…I'm still waitlisted…I mean…" My head is spinning. Is he really trying to *buy* my pregnancy? I finally come out with, "No, thank you."

"I'm disappointed," he says. "I thought we were on the same page."

"I just need to think about it," I repeat. Dumb like a parrot, but at least I'm holding my ground.

The silence on the other end is so long, I think he's ended the call. Then he finally says, "I'll schedule a new appointment. I'd recommend you make this one."

I hang up immediately. My hands are shaking, and I can't catch my breath, like I'm breathing through a straw. I lie down on the hardwood floor and close my eyes until the spinning stops.

* * *

"Are you avoiding me?"

I look up, and there he is. The man I *have* been avoiding. Jason King.

In the grocery store, of all places.

It takes a minute for my mouth to work. Pearl is down the opposite aisle, and I stand there, like an idiot, with a jar of peanut butter in my hand, which I've been debating for the past five minutes because *why* this sudden craving for peanut butter?

He's leaning against my shopping cart, wearing a green bomber jacket and a crooked grin. And…*goddammit.*

Two weeks of carefully crafted avoidance wasn't long enough. The very sight of his tall frame, his dark hair, and mischievous blue eyes makes me flutter.

More than anything, in the sweets aisle of the grocery store, I want to grab his stupid, beautiful face and feel the warmth of his lips on mine.

But I don't. Instead, I scoff, throwing up my walls. "Don't you have like…a personal chef to do the shopping for you?"

He shrugs. "Most of the time. But she never buys…"—he pulls a box from the shelf—"*Gushers.*"

I can't help the grin that lifts my lips. I missed his terrible sense of humor.

"Jason!" A voice barks his name, and he winces.

"Also," he adds, "my dad is really picky about his cuts of steak."

My heart freezes. *Mr. King is here.*

My whole body goes numb. I shove the peanut butter away and grab the shopping cart. "I actually should find Pearl, we're kind of on a time crunch…"

"Hold up." He grips the rim of the shopping cart, and he's too strong for me to yank it back. "Answer my question first."

I sigh dramatically. "What. Something about Gushers?"

"No. Are you avoiding me?"

When those blue eyes meet mine…part of my chest caves in. For someone so tall, he looks suddenly small. Vulnerable.

"Did I do something wrong?" he asks.

Words coming up like acid in my throat. I want to tell him. I'm *going* to tell him. He deserves to know.

But then, down the aisle, I see him approaching. Mr. King. His eyes land on me, and they narrow.

I have to get out of here. My voice is sharp, my teeth are chattering, and what comes flying out of my mouth next is the only thing I can think of to get him to leave: "Jesus, Jason, it was just a summer fling. Man up."

I yank the shopping cart, and this time, he releases his grip. He looks kicked. But I'm running on adrenaline now—no turning back now. I exit the aisle and push the cart forward, away, trying to find Pearl, trying to get out of here…

Trying to ignore the tears blurring my vision, or the metallic taste of shame in my mouth.

* * *

I open the jar of peanut butter on the way back to Four's. I eat it with my fingers. It lumps in my mouth and my throat, and I take no joy in it, but I keep shoveling it back anyway.

Pearl parks the car out front and then hops out. "Can you get the rest of the bags, darling?" she calls out.

But "rest of" she means "all of," but I don't complain. It takes me a second to suck the sweet stickiness from my fingers, but then I screw the jar shut and get to work. I clamber out of the car and load the groceries onto my arms. All my movements feel slow. Every task is a chore.

I want to curl under the blankets of my bed and sleep for a year.

I use my foot to kick the car door closed and trudge inside. Except my bad mood doesn't get to linger, because the second I open the door—

"Surprise!"

For a minute, I just stare at the sight in front of me. There's a colored banner hanging across the wall with the word "Congratulations!" Four and Pearl are standing side by side, staring at me, all wide, toothy smiles. A single cupcake sits on a plate on the table, a candle in it.

First, I think, *It's not my birthday.*

Then, it hits me. They must have found out about the baby. And they're…happy about it?

"We're so proud of you, kid," Four says, really laying on the dad-role thick.

Proud of me? This isn't how I thought this conversation would go. My mouth is dry. Maybe from nerves. Maybe from all the peanut butter I devoured in the car. I drop the grocery bags to the floor.

"Um. Thanks. How did you…find out?"

"We got the letter," Pearl says.

The letter?

She then whisks a letter off the foyer and holds it out for me. It's folded in three places, and I have to flatten it out.

Ms. Kenzi Stratton,

We're delighted to inform you that you've been accepted to…

"Holy shit," I gasp. "I'm off the waitlist."

I reread the letter. Twice.

"I'm going to Berklee!"

Pearl lets out a whoop, and Four pulls out a noisemaker from who knows where and blows into it.

For the first time in weeks, I'm grinning ear to ear. My mom wraps her arms around me, and I find myself clinging to her, crushing her against me.

"I knew you'd do it, darling," she says.

I bury my face in her shoulder and fight off tears that have been welling up all day.

"That's all it takes," Four goes off, his voice meandering. "Hard work. Patience. And a little angel on your shoulder."

I release Pearl from my death-grip hug. "What angel?" I ask

Four looks pleased with himself. "I had lunch with the Kings the other day. I mentioned to him that you were wait-listed. Leonard said he'd look into it. I didn't think anything of it at the time, but, well…"

"Well," I echo. My heart is a balloon, deflating.

"It seems Leonard put in a good word for you after all," Four says.

An angel on my shoulders…or a devil.

"Oh, isn't that nice?" Pearl muses.

I feel like I swallowed a rock. My one bubble of hope, this precious moment that I could finally hold on to, now sullied.

The Kings giveth. The Kings taketh away.

I know what this is: a small taste of the power he wields. It's like Donovan said—the only thing Mr. King wants is *control.*

Just like his son, Mr. King is persistent. I'm an inconvenience. A black mark on his son's otherwise perfect record. And he'll never stop until I give him exactly what he wants.

He'll follow me. To college. Anywhere I go.

The knowledge is dizzying, and I sway on my feet. This room is suddenly too tiny. Pearl and Four are too close. My very *bones* itch.

"I…have to pee," I lie. "I'll be right back."

"The cupcake!" Pearl's voice pitches.

I quickly blow out the candle, take a bite off the top, and shout, "It's delicious!" before rushing upstairs to the bathroom.

I lock the door, close the toilet lid, and sit on it.

I have to make a choice. And I have to make it fast.

KENZI

I can't sleep. I lie awake, staring at the ceiling.

Every now and then, I glance at the window. I think part of me keeps hoping Jason will climb through it again. That I'll run off with him and Donovan to someplace where no one will ever find us. We could take Donovan's boat. Leave and never come back.

Wishful thinking. But when I touch my belly, tracing the place where there's a seed of *something* springing to life, I know that they're just that. *Wishes.*

I climb out of bed. I shuffle down the hall to where Pearl and Four share a room. When I open the door a crack, I can see them in bed together, washed in nighttime blue. Four is snoring loudly. Pearl—somehow—is fast asleep in her nightie beside him.

Which, on closer inspection, probably has something to do with the earplugs in her ears, the eye mask covering her eyes, and the sound machine going beside her bed. Not to mention whatever sleeping aid she took with a wine chaser.

There's a good chance a herd of elephants wouldn't wake her up, but it's worth a shot.

I stand about a foot from her bed, holding my arm awkwardly like an injured animal, and gently try: "Mom?"

Maybe it's the rarely used M-O-M word that activates some primitive response in her brain, overriding all else. Immediately, she stirs, peeling up her sleep mask and peeking at me with one bleary eye.

"Kenzi? What's wrong, darling?"

"It's…um. I have something to tell you."

"What is it?"

But the words are stuck. A lump in the back of my throat.

Pearl sits up and pats the mattress beside her. "Come. Sit."

I do. She winds her arms around me, and I crawl into her. I curl up in her lap and sniffle. I don't want to be eighteen. I want to be eight. No, younger. I want to be a fetus, curled up inside my mother's womb.

"Oh, darling," she murmurs, "whatever it is, we'll figure it out. I promise."

That breaks the dam. I tell her.

Everything.

KENZI

onovan,

Hey. I suck at letters. So this is going to suck. That's got to be something with our generation, right? No one writes letters anymore. I feel like I should be writing this with a quill by candlelight or something. Haha.

Anyway. Pearl and I are leaving Hannsett Island today. I'm sorry I didn't get to see you. Everything just happened really fast. It's hard to explain right now. I WANT to explain it. Of all people, I want to talk to you. Tell you everything. And I will. One day.

Don't stress. It's good, I think.

The point of this letter is this: this has been one of the best, wildest summers of my life. For the first time, I felt like I fit in my own skin. And I feel like that's all because of you. You're one of the bravest guys I know. You're YOU, unapologetically. Even when it's hard. Especially when it's hard. I admire that. Never change.

Keep being you. Keep being amazing. You were my

favorite part of the summer and I hope I was, at least, a bright spot on yours.

Tell Jason I'm sorry. Tell your dad he's raised a good kid. Tell that muskrat…squeak-squeak.

Maybe we'll find each other, ten years from now, and laugh about all of this.

xoxo,
Kenzi

GRAB THE SEQUEL!

I hope you enjoyed The Bully's Dare! Find out what happens next when Kenzi, Jason & Donovan are all grown up in The Doctor's Truth.

Buy now on Amazon!

At 18, I lost my v-card to my two best friends. And then came the fall out.

I ran from Hannsett Island. It's been me and my son against the world ever since.

I told myself I'd never go back, but my son is sick. And the two doctors who could save his life...?

Jason and Donovan. The same two boys I shared one hot, steamy night with over ten years ago.

Can I keep my secret safe...even though it threatens to slip out every time their lips touch mine?

Keep reading for a preview...

The Doctor's Truth

A SPICY WHY CHOOSE ROMANCE

USA TODAY BESTSELLING AUTHOR

ADORA CROOKS

1

KENZI

When I was thirteen, my mother sat me down and taught me a very important lesson. "Men," she said, "are only good for two things. Money and sex."

And she should know—she'd been married and divorced three times by that point. She's since doubled the number.

"What about love?" I'd asked, still pimply-faced and doe-eyed.

"Love yourself, darling," she told me as she refilled her goldfish-bowl-size glass of merlot. "Only you can do that."

I take her advice to heart. As I grew up, *loving myself* took on a very physical meaning.

With the stress of my job as a publicist for a pop rock band and no viable men on the horizon, I found only one thing helped me get through the hard times.

Reliable, trustworthy Burtie.

Burtie—named after my first crush, Burt Reynolds—is a pink, long vibrator. He twists. He has ridges. He makes my toes curl in a way no man ever can.

He's also the reason why I'm late to my gate at Heathrow Airport.

The security guard taps my bag. "Is this yours, miss?"

"Yes, it is."

"I'm going to have to take a look inside."

I fidget. I'm bundled up, sweating uncomfortably under two sweaters, a jacket, and a huge backpack. I wish I'd thought to bring a hair tie, because long, static strands of black hair keep getting stuck to my mouth and covering my eyes.

"Okay…I mean, I think I know what the issue is if you just want me to take it out…"

When I reach for my bag, however, he pulls it closer to him and gives me a glare. "Miss, please step back," he says. The security guard has a crew cut and a bulldog's frown, so I take him seriously.

"Okay," I try, "but…"

He unzips my backpack and pushes his gloved hand inside of it. He nudges around a moment, and the bag starts *humming*.

Oh boy. Here we go…

His eyebrow arches. He pulls out Burtie, who vibrates helplessly in the guard's hand.

"I can explain this," I start, when I feel a small human nudge against my legs.

"Mum! We've gotta go!"

Otto, my twelve-year-old, is a bundle of nerves and anxiety on a normal day, but today, his type A personality is really bursting out of its skin. He wears a bulky helmet, and he takes a break from adjusting the strap under his chin to tug on my pants.

Quickly, I cover his eyes with my hand. "Look," I reason with the security guard, "it's not like I was going to *use* it on the plane, but little man here likes to go through the luggage, so—"

"Just take out the batteries," he says, clearly eager to move on to any *non*-sex-obsessed single mom.

And, really, I'm *not* addicted to sex. I can count the

number of times I've gotten laid in the past decade on one hand.

So is it a crime to need a little...*help*...every now and then?

I shove Burtie deep in my bag, pop out the batteries, and zip up my bag so we can book it to the gate.

2

KENZI

It takes an eight-hour flight, a three-hour drive, and a thirty-minute ferry ride to get to Hannsett Island.

I'm feeling the thick fog of jet lag in my skull, but I grip the steering wheel of my rental car, a white PT Cruiser, and knuckle through it. Otto, who slept most of the flight, is now bouncing around excitedly, face pressed against the glass.

"Mum! Look at all the snow! It's like a gingerbread town!"

"Yeah, baby," I murmur. "Just like a gingerbread town."

The last time I was here, over a decade ago, it was a different picture. Summer. Hot sun, crystal-white beaches, kids playing volleyball in the sand.

It's winter now. December 17, to be exact. And Hannsett Island is a ghost town. The tourists, like geese, flew elsewhere for the winter, leaving nothing but locals with parkas and shovels behind. The sun dips low in the sky now, bleeding out a red winter sunset, and the lights flicker on along Main Street. Streetlamps are tethered with holly and Christmas lights. There are a couple of signs of life—a lantern flickering outside of a tavern that calls itself "The

Anchor" and, bizarrely, an ice cream shop—but most of the storefronts look locked down for the winter.

The road is slick, snow drifting softly, and I drive slowly, not putting too much faith in my Cruiser's capabilities.

As we climb the small incline up the island, the Lighthouse Medical Center comes into view. It's a large, multi-building medical center, connected to an old red lighthouse by the edge of the cliff, which gives it its name.

Hannsett Island has two main draws: the sparkling beaches in the summer and Lighthouse Medical, which is known as one of the most prominent medical centers in the Northeast. And, unsurprisingly, one of the most expensive and hardest to get into. The waiting list is a year out.

I know. I've checked. And I don't have a year to spare.

"Are we almost there?" Otto whines. "I'm tired."

"I know, me too, honey. We just have one more errand to run, and then we'll be done for the night, okay?"

"Okay," he grumbles.

I don't blame him for wanting to go to sleep. I want to sleep, too. Hell, I want to do anything *except* for what I'm about to do. It's risky, it's insane, and borderline illegal.

But I've got nothing left to lose.

I find the parking lot at the back of the center and park the car. Otto and I climb out, and he follows me inside. It's freezing outside, and we're met with a gush of hot air as soon as the sliding doors open for us. A statue sits in the lobby—a man holding up the universe. *A guiding light through the dark* reads the inscription, and I really hope it's true.

I head to the front desk and pull on my nicest smile. "Hi!"

The receptionist is probably twenty minutes from clocking out, but she pulls a polite smile for me all the same. "How can I help you?"

"My name is Kenzi Stratton. I'm here to see Mr. Leonard King."

The edge of her mouth slides downward into a frown.

"I'm sorry...he's packing up for the day. Did you have an appointment?"

"Not exactly, but it's really important that I see him."

Her eyes fall to Otto, who is laying his helmet-head on the counter, looking tired. I shift my body between them to get her attention. *Look at me, don't look at my kid.* "I'm with the *Dr. Mazie Show*," I lie. "Maybe you've heard of it?"

"Oh!" Her eyes light up suddenly, excited. "Yes, I *love* that show. This must be about Jason's appearance?"

"Sure is."

She presses her lips together, thinking about it, though she's clearly made up her mind already. "His office is on the top floor, to the left. If you go now, you might still be able to catch him."

"Thank you."

I quickly grab Otto's hand and lead him to the elevator. He lets me drag him along, and we pile into the elevator.

I press the button and wait. In the metallic walls, I can half see my reflection. My thick black hair looks knotted, and I push my hands over my shirt and pants to remove any wrinkles. I wore a blazer underneath the bulky sweaters I left in the car, and I'm hoping it hides the massive sweat stains that are growing around my pits.

"How do I look?" I ask Otto.

"Like twenty bucks," he assures me.

"Don't you mean a million?"

"No. I mean twenty."

The elevator doors swing open. The hallways are white, nondescript, and I follow the receptionist's instructions and hang a left. There's a lot of empty conference rooms on this floor, the walls layered with glass, and luxury suite hospital rooms. I come to a stop at a door marked *Dr. Leonard King, CEO*.

The shutters hang down around his glass walls, but I can still see a light glowing from inside. There are a couple of chairs in the hallway, and I guide Otto to sit down in one.

"Can you sit here for ten minutes? I'll be right in that room if you need me."

"Okay…and then we can go to bed?"

"And then we can go to bed."

He has a ketchup stain on his button-up shirt, and I lick my thumb and wipe the stain. He makes a face that says *Mum, stop messing with me.*

"You're my bacon," I tell him.

"You're mine," he replies.

No way but forward. I go to the door, take a deep breath. *You can do this.*

No way but forward. I knock on the door and hear a low "Come in."

So I turn the handle and enter.

There's dark carpet on the floors and a beautiful view of the lighthouse outside the large floor-to-ceiling windows.

At a stained-oak desk sits Leonard King himself. He's gotten older since I last saw him—the salt-and-pepper look graduated to a full-on gray beard and white-tipped sideburns.

Still handsome, though. The kind of wrinkled face they only make in Hollywood. Piercing blue eyes, just like his son. Just like his *grandson.*

He has a pair of reading glasses on, and he's examining papers on his desk. When I step inside, he looks up at me from underneath thick eyebrows and narrows his eyes.

"Hi…Mr. King?"

"How can I help you?" Not unfriendly, but curt. To the point. A man who doesn't have time for small talk.

I force myself forward and extend my hand. "Kenzi Stratton. It's been…thirteen years now?"

He takes my hand. Shakes it. "I'm sorry. I meet a lot of patients."

"It's okay. I don't expect you to remember me…last time we met, I was eighteen and pregnant, and you were trying to buy off my baby."

His smile falters. He releases my hand and immediately straightens up in his seat. The color falls from his face, but, to his credit, he keeps his composure, his mouth a thin line. "That's not quite how I remember it."

"No problem—I'll refresh your memory." I drop my purse down on his desk and invite myself into the plush chair across from him. He doesn't move a muscle—I'm not sure he's even breathing, honestly. "August 2005. A precocious, geeky teenager spends the summer on glorious Hannsett Island. Meets a charming, cocky boy—that's your son, Jason King—and decides to lose her virginity. Three positive pregnancy tests later, she comes to you looking for help. You tell her—this scared, eighteen-year-old girl—that it would be better if the pregnancy didn't exist and that you'll help her *take care of it*. You bribe her. Threaten her. And then she and her mother vanish in the wind. Are you following me so far?"

His jaw is so tight, and there's a vein crawling up the side of his forehead, protruding. "What do you want?"

"I want you to take a peek out your window."

He leans over and parts the shutters between his fingers. "What am I looking at?"

"The boy in the chair? That's my son…your grandchild. Otto Stratton. Twelve years old and the best kid in the world."

Those blue eyes turn to me. "If you want money…"

Anger lashes through me, rising up like bile, and it takes everything within me to contain it. "I don't *want* your money. We've been doing just fine on our own." I take in a small sip of breath. Controlled. "Otto is sick. He has been for a while now."

Mr. King steeples his fingers together. "I'm sorry to hear that."

"No. You're not. Trust me, I wouldn't be here if I had any other options." I'm sweating. I'm shaking. But I can't stop now. Not when I'm so close to what I want. "I want you to admit him. Here. He deserves the best care."

Mr. King leans back in his chair. He takes his time, now that our seesawing power play has swung his way momentarily. "And if I say no?" he asks.

"Then I tell my story to all of Jason's new friends and fans." Now my trump card, I pull out my phone and turn it to face Mr. King. I click the thumbnail, and the video plays.

* * *

Want to find out what happens next? Continue reading with "The Doctor's Truth!"

ABOUT THE AUTHOR

USA Today bestselling author Adora Crooks writes romance with heart, action, humor, and steam. Here, you can find love stories that are larger than life, kick-ass heroines, and the strong, brooding men who crave them. She primarily writes MMF stories (or ménage romances with m/m scenes), but also writes m/f as well.

A former New Yorker, she currently resides in the magical city of New Orleans with her beloved and their two nutty mutts. Adora lives off of coffee, cookies, and book reviews and daydreams about dirty romances with happy-ever-afters.

Join her newsletter to download a free romance  https://adoracrooksbooks.com/gift

Follow Adora Crooks https://adoracrooksbooks.com/follow-me/

ALSO BY ADORA CROOKS

MMF Ménage & LGBTQ+ Romance

The Royal's Love (Complete Series)

Rory is a lone American vlogging her way through England. When she goes home with the attractive stranger from the bar, she doesn't expect him to be the prince's bodyguard…or for the prince to join in. When their menage a trois goes viral, sh*t really hits the fan.

Mr. Hollywood's Secret

Eric North is Hollywood's favorite leading man. But he has a secret: his boyfriend, Nico. When his agent sets him up with a fake fiancee, the chemistry between all three of them is very real.

M/F Romance

<u>The Best Man Wins</u>

She s a wedding planner with her career on the line. He's the best man determined to break up the engagement before the couple says their vows. It's a battle to the final "I do."

Protecting His Finch

She's trapped as the ward of a mafia family. He's the older bodyguard who has protected her for years. Can they escape the family and find peace together?